# End In Flames

## TRACY BROEMMER

End in Flames

by


Tracy Broemmer

Contemporary Romance Novella


Published by Tracy Broemmer

Edited by Lexie Broemmer

Cover Photo: Deposit Photos

Cover Design by Designed With Grace

Copyright: © 2022

ISBN#: 978-1-951637-43-9

# END IN FLAMES

https://bit.ly/RescueMeHeroCollection

# CHAPTER
# ONE

B en Sager woke to the sounds of *Paw Patrol* coming from the other room. He rolled his head on his pillow—well, technically Heather's pillow—only to find her side of the bed empty.

*Dammit.*

He'd come over late when he shouldn't have. Exhausted after his shift ended, he should have gone straight home. But big bad fireman that he was, his empty apartment was the last damned place he wanted to be. So, he'd exercised his selfish muscle and gone to his ex-wife's house in search of sympathy. A little TLC.

Not *that* kind. They'd made that mistake last weekend. A few too many longnecks. Heather in that oversized gray shirt that was always sliding off her shoulder. Ben's dick like a fucking battering ram when she finished the last of her bottle and put it down. That look on her face. The bold lust in her eyes.

Naomi had been at Heather's sister's house for the evening, so why not fall on each other and strip down to

1

skin and fuck like kids on the couch? The way they used to. Before Heather graduated from college and started the forty hour a week job at Pennington Seed. Before he had walked into a burning building the first time and before he had dragged a body out of a burning building.

Before he was dead inside.

Before Naomi.

*Naomi.*

How the hell was he going to explain to his three-year-old why he had slept in Mommy's bed? Well, he wasn't going to explain it, because you didn't reason with a three-year-old. But still, seeing her daddy walk out of Mommy's bedroom after a year of not having her daddy around would confuse her.

Why hadn't Heather woken him? He could have slipped out before Naomi was awake. Ben rubbed his eyes as he rolled to his side and sat up. With a quiet groan, he leaned forward to prop his elbows on his knees, still wearing the same dark sweats he'd worn when he came by last night.

Heather had fed him. He'd guzzled a beer but stopped after that first one. Sat on the living room floor with Naomi and played along with her imaginary tea party.

He told himself he would leave after Heather put Naomi to bed, but Heather had taken his hand and led him to her bedroom. While fucking her last weekend had been as incredible as every other time they had been together—sex had never been their problem—he hadn't been in the mood for it last night. His back hurt. The hammering pain in the back of his skull had only lessened a bit when he played with Naomi. He tried to beg off.

She shushed him, led him to the bed, and gave him a gentle shove. When his dick finally responded to her standing over him at the side of the bed, Heather rolled her eyes.

"Turn over."

Those were the last words she had said to him. Instead of initiating sex, she had straddled his ass cheeks and reached for the drawer in the nightstand. Ben saw her pull a bottle of massage oil from the drawer. For a second, a petulant wave of jealousy rolled over him, threatening to drown him. They'd been divorced for a year. And they were divorced because he was a cold-hearted SOB who drifted away from his wife in favor of bottles—brown, clear, short and fat, longneck. Didn't matter.

He'd picked a girl up at a bar a month or two after the divorce. That lasted a few weeks. She wasn't Heather. He wasn't what she wanted. End of story. Until last weekend with Heather, the only action his dick got was his hand, but that didn't mean Heather hadn't found someone else. And it didn't matter how badly Ben hated wondering about her with another man, she had every right to move on.

Her hands. The dark room. The oil. The bed. Something had worked on him. He didn't even remember her climbing off him. Going to sleep. Hell, maybe she hadn't woken him because she hadn't slept next to him. Maybe she had left him in her room and slept in their daughter's little pink toddler bed with her.

Ben twisted around and looked back at her side of the bed, her nightshirt tossed over her pillow. Still uncertain, he stood and made his way to the en suite bathroom. Closed and locked the door, because sweet little Naomi knew no boundaries. He stood at the toilet with his sweats and briefs shoved down out of the way and waited a few moments for the morning wood to ease so he could piss.

Coffee would be nice, but he still wasn't sure how to play this with Naomi. There wouldn't be any discussion —no *Daddy wasn't feeling well and fell asleep in Mommy's bed.* But would Naomi wake tomorrow and remember that he'd been here today and come looking for him? Christ, he hoped not. He'd done enough to mess his kid up already just by leaving her and her mother.

When he finished, he washed his hands quickly, avoiding his face in the mirror. Back in the bedroom, he found the t-shirt he had worn last night on the floor by the bed and snatched it to pull it on. His shoulders and back did feel looser. The headache had quieted to a dull roar for now.

Tiptoeing down the hall, he found Naomi in front of the TV, wispy brown hair floating around her head like a cloud and her stuffed frog at her side. Ben looked around for Heather and moved slowly through the living room to the kitchen when he heard her making breakfast.

She glanced at him over her shoulder when she heard him. With her hair pinned up in a messy twist and another oversized shirt on, Ben had to remind himself to stay away from her. They weren't good together, and together, they weren't good for Naomi. He loved them too much to keep dragging Heather back into his cold heart.

"Why didn't you wake me?"

"Because it's not even seven," she answered quietly. "I thought you could use some sleep."

Ben peeked at the round clock on the wall with a frown.

"Does she always get up this early?"

"Yes." Heather nodded with a soft snort of laughter. "Want a waffle?"

"No, thanks." Ben clapped his hand around the back of his neck and then ruffled his fingers up over the back of his hair. "I should get outta here."

Her lack of reaction told him she agreed with him.

"Thanks." He touched her upper arm. "For the...massage."

"Yeah." She shrugged, but she didn't look at him.

"We didn't—?"

Heather shot him a look as a rumble of laughter bubbled out of her.

"No. Not last night."

He grinned, a little relieved and a little sad. "I must have been beat. I don't even remember you...stopping."

"You were out." She pulled Naomi's waffle from the toaster and dropped it on a plate.

"Look." He cleared his throat. "I'm sorry. About last week—"

"Don't, Ben." She met his eyes with a bold stare, not unlike the one she had given him last weekend. "We're adults. We had sex."

He stared at her for a moment longer and finally

nodded. She was right. Neither of them was anymore to blame than the other.

"What do I say to Naomi?"

He stopped at the doorway and looked back at Heather.

She shrugged as she buttered the waffle.

"She's not gonna know you came out of the bedroom if she didn't see you."

Ben nodded and left Heather in the kitchen. Naomi glanced at him, did a doubletake, and then climbed to her feet to fling herself at him.

"Daddy!"

"Hey, Princess."

"She's not a princess," Heather called from the kitchen. "She's a tough dragon slayer."

Ben kissed Naomi's cheek and tickled her belly. "Is that true? Are you a dragon slayer?"

His little girl beamed at him and nodded. Naomi was the only thing in his world right now that he had done right. Ben was determined to be a good dad, even though he'd bombed as a husband.

# TWO

Indigo and vermillion streaked the evening sky. Carlie Beringer shivered as she crossed the parking lot as fast as her wedge heels would allow. In protest against the dropping temperatures and the end of daylight-saving time that fell on the upcoming weekend, she had left her jacket in her Honda when she arrived at work that morning. Naturally, she regretted it now.

Still when she reached her car, she stood for a moment and looked around. She did love fall; the changing of the leaves in her hometown was what kept her right there in the Midwest. Across the street from the strip mall that housed Wanderlust—the travel agency where she had worked the past three years—the bank courtyard boasted a couple of Elm trees aflame in yellows and oranges.

If only it would stay like this. A bit brisk in the mornings, maybe a chilly breeze. No snow, no ice. Carlie dreaded winter as much as she loved fall. At least she had her beach vacation to look forward to. One more day of work, and then she and her best friend Erin were heading to Florida.

The thought of day drinking on the beach with her bestie stirred her into action. Carlie unlocked her door and slid into the driver's seat, still lost in thought about the trip. She and Erin had gone to Colorado a few months ago for an extended weekend. They'd had a great time, though they had been there in the off-season and hadn't done any skiing. Carlie planned to go back soon to enjoy the slopes.

Turning her radio up a bit, she backed out of her spot and headed east. She needed to stock up on a few travel items. Rather than rush tomorrow after she got off work, she decided to go tonight. That way she could pack after work tomorrow and spend the rest of her evening with Nash, her Aussie-German Shepherd. If the weather wasn't too bad, she would walk him over to see her brother and his wife before she left town.

Carlie didn't mind the drive across town to shop. After all, in less than forty-eight hours, she and Erin would be in Florida. Traveling was part of her job. She researched fun locales—some well-known and some off the beaten path—online and in travel magazines, and when she found something that looked interesting to her, she took the idea to her bosses and pitched it. Sometimes, her ideas were shot down, but not always.

While traveling, she took loads of pictures—landscapes, candid shots of strangers, though she was careful not to get close-ups of faces, and even shots of herself and Erin—and she made thorough notes about every part of the trip: the airport and flight experience, the accommodations, and the actual adventures, of course. After a few trips, her bosses had suggested she write a blog for their website and catalog. The trips were incredible experiences, and the blog was proving to be insightful and beloved by their clientele.

She slowed as she approached her turn and flipped her signal on. The sunset in the rearview mirror caught her eye for a second; she wished she had taken a picture of it with her phone before she'd left work.

When Carlie turned her attention back to the road in front of her, a black SUV was barreling straight at her. For a second, she panicked, worried that she had wavered over the center line, but a quick look around told her she was stopped in her own lane, turn signal on, and waiting for a break in traffic to execute her turn.

The black SUV had crossed the line. Carlie held her breath as the grill of the vehicle smashed into hers. A distant shriek sounded in her ears, and then her world went black.

# THREE

The heap of crumpled metal in the middle of the four-lane road turned Ben's stomach. Once upon a time, he'd thrived on this stuff. Not misfortune. But the chance to do the impossible and help someone in need.

Adrenaline pumped through his body, driving his heartrate up. At least that part of him still worked. He still had the drive to fight natural and manmade disasters. He still wanted to *help* people. He just didn't give a damn about himself anymore, he supposed.

Two cop cars sat at an angle, one on each side of the wreck. Ben saw a uniform a hundred feet up the road, light in hand, directing traffic around the scene. Bozeman stopped the rig as close to the accident as he could without disturbing anything. He cut the siren and left the lights on as Ben and the rest of the crew jumped down from the truck to the pavement. Ben surveyed the crunched vehicles for a moment from where he stood and then rushed closer to get a handle on the victims.

The male driver of the black SUV had been thrown

from the vehicle. Ben saw Bozeman and Fisher attending to him, Bozeman looking back over his shoulder as the ambo roared up behind them. Ben hurried around to the driver's side of the other car. The front end of the small SUV was completely bashed in, the hood folded accordion-style, and the windshield cracked in a spiderweb design.

Ben squatted a bit to peer into the driver's side window. A mess of blond hair mostly covered the driver's face, but Ben could make out a cheekbone and an eyebrow. He knocked on the closed window.

"Ma'am? Ma'am, can you hear me?"

At first there was no movement, but he knocked again. This time, he saw the woman's fingers flex just a bit on the steering wheel.

"Ma'am?" He knocked harder this time, and the woman rolled her head on the seat to look at him. Two things hit Ben immediately. One—she was young. She looked like a kid fresh out of high school. Two—blood. The left side of her face was streaked with blood from an open gash in her hairline.

"Can you hear me?" he yelled through the glass.

Ben took a deep, steadying breath as he met her wide, frightened eyes.

"Can you open the door?" he tried again. A slow blink but no other response. Hand on the closed window, Ben looked the SUV over. The front panel was pushed back to buckle the door. He slipped his fingers around the handle and tugged, but it didn't budge.

"I'm gonna help you," he called to the girl. "Hang in there. I'll be right back!"

Her lips were still parted, but she only stared.

"Gonna need the shears over here!" he yelled as he backed away from the Jeep. Forsythe was already heading his way with the jaws of life in his hand.

"What've we got?" The older man yelled over the roar of the truck engine.

"Too soon to know," Ben answered. "Front panel's buckled, and the door's jammed. She's got a head injury. Can't tell anything else yet."

"Okay."

Those dazed brown eyes and the blood streaking her face inspired Ben to act. He took the shears from Forsythe and stepped closer to the SUV again to assure the girl that she would be okay. Panic seized him when he saw her eyes were closed.

He rapped his knuckles on the window again, but she didn't move.

"Ma'am?" he called. "Can you hear me?"

Her fingers flinched again. Ben studied the steering wheel for a second and realized finally that it was shoved into her lap. Odds were, one—maybe both—of her legs were broken. Before he could wonder if she was a dancer or an athlete, he turned his attention back to the tool in his hand.

A cold wind whipped up around him as he and Forsythe worked to free the girl from the wreckage. The claw-like end of the lifesaving tool snipped the car door post, and Bozeman and Fisher rushed over to help peel the top of the SUV back.

The girl blinked again once she was exposed to the weather. Without the metal trappings of the wreckage,

Ben could see she was indeed pinned in place by the dash of the SUV, the steering wheel shoved into her lap. The airbag hadn't gone off, and she had hit her head.

"Can you hear me?" Ben said again. Forsythe and Fisher pulled the remains of the driver's door away, leaving Ben full access to the victim.

She worked her mouth to speak but gave up and tried to shake her head. Ben felt her tiny shriek of pain in his gut.

"Try not to move, okay?" He touched her hand. "There's another ambulance on the way."

She whispered something, but the words barely made it past her lips. Ben crouched at her side and leaned in.

"Say it again."

"I can't..."

He watched her struggle to swallow, to breathe again so she could continue.

"Feel. I can't...my legs."

"You can't feel your legs," he confirmed. She licked her lips and nodded her head the tiniest bit.

"It's okay," he promised her. "You've got a lot going on right now. We're gonna get you to the hospital. Doctors are gonna fix you up, okay?"

"...hurts..."

Her voice was thick with pain, heavy with exhaustion. Ben had no idea what she had said hurt, but he was willing to bet every inch of her body hurt like hell.

"I know, sweetheart," he crooned. Obviously, the girl was older than Naomi, but he had a flash of his own daughter broken and bleeding in a life-threatening situation. This girl needed her family with her. He looked over at the passenger seat, wondering if she had a purse with her.

"Someone who witnessed the accident said the other driver was texting."

Ben flinched when he heard Bozeman speak.

"Bozeman." Ben looked over his shoulder at his colleague. "Search over there for a purse. Let's find some ID and get this kid some support."

"On it."

Ben turned his attention back to the girl in the driver's seat. She watched him with wide eyes.

"Can you tell me your name?"

She licked her lips again and closed her eyes.

"Stay with me, sweetheart." He closed his fingers around her hand and gave her a gentle squeeze. "Look at me."

On the other side of the car, Bozeman found an upended black bag on the floorboard. From the corner of his eye, Ben saw him searching through the items that had fallen out, looking for a billfold or driver's license.

"Erin's..."

"Erin?" he repeated. "Your name's Erin?"

"Destin." She swallowed hard. "Call her...I can't. No way."

"Erin?" Ben squeezed her hand again. "Sweetheart, I'm Ben. I'm gonna wait right here with you until the ambulance gets here, okay?"

She blinked again.

"What happened?"

"You had a bit of an accident," Ben told her. "We're

gonna get you patched up. Just hang in there with me, okay?"

"Hurts."

"I know, Erin—"

She shook her head quickly and yelped with pain. Fresh blood glistened in the gash on her head.

"No."

"No what?"

"Erin." She pressed her lips together and squeezed her eyes closed. "I'm not. I'm not Erin."

"Oh." Ben nodded. "Aaron? Are you asking for Aaron?"

"Mmm."

The girl sank her teeth into her lower lip and groaned softly.

"Stay with me," Ben said again.

"We were going to..." She blinked and looked at him again. "Do you pray?"

Ben stared at the girl, dumbfounded. He didn't. Not since Heather had given birth to Naomi, and it had hit him that somewhere up there some higher power had given him the greatest blessing in the world.

"Will you pray?" she whispered.

"I don't—"

He had been taught the Our Father as a kid, but damned if he remembered much beyond the opening *Our Father.*

"I can't feel my legs," she whispered again. This time when she closed her eyes, silent tears slipped over her cheeks. "And I can't...I can't breathe."

"Pray." Ben squeezed her hand again.

When she whispered *Our Father*, Ben ducked his head and searched his memory to join her in prayer. He pulled to mind the fire two years ago when an older man had escaped and fallen to his knees to pray for the wife who didn't make it out of the house safely. He echoed the girl's words and pulled the old man's words back and refused to let his personal demons interfere.

The whoop of the second ambo's siren finally registered in his head as the kid closed the prayer.

Broken legs. Spinal injuries. Broken ribs. Punctured lungs.

Ben considered all the possibilities as Traeder and Dawson rushed toward the mangled vehicle with a stretcher. The girl's eyes flew open, and she stared at Ben wildly as he climbed to his feet.

"Don't leave." Her broken whisper sounded more like a sob.

"My friends here are gonna take care of you, sweetheart," he promised her.

"Please."

When he felt the slight pressure on his hand, Ben looked down and realized she had twined her fingers with his.

"I'm right here," he promised her. "But I need to let my friends get you outta the car. Okay?"

# CHAPTER

# FOUR

B en wondered about the girl—Bozeman had finally found her ID—several times through his shift, but when his truck was called out to a small house fire and another—less serious—car accident, he had to shove those thoughts aside.

According to her Illinois issued driver's license, Carlie Beringer was twenty-five. Ben spent a few moments thinking about that, surprised to learn she wasn't younger. He wondered, too, about Aaron, if the boyfriend had been contacted. If he was the type who would stick around when the going got tough.

He had two more full days before he was off shift, so he threw himself into drills and chores to pass the time. He told himself he stayed busy to keep the kid out of his mind, and yet, while he was busy with mundane things, he found himself wondering how she was doing.

When his fourth day ended, he went home for a shower. Normally, he checked in with Heather via phone call, but he texted her this time and asked after Naomi.

He left his phone in the kitchen and took a longneck to the closet-sized bathroom with him, fully aware of what he was doing. Blowing his ex-wife off in favor of a cold beer and a hot shower. The sort of thing that had led to Heather being his ex.

He would call. Of course, he would call to check on Naomi. But first he would shower and down the beer. And maybe sleep. He hadn't been able to rest at the station. Every time he closed his eyes, he pictured Carlie Beringer's face. Her big doe-like eyes.

His apartment sucked compared to the house he had shared with Heather. His bathroom—particularly the shower—was the worst of it. Still, being home, alone, was therapeutic, even if his elbows did bump the walls when he moved. His body hurt some from the job. Some days were worse than others. Ben considered that the young woman in the SUV accident might not walk again as he scrubbed his hair. He had no right to complain. Hell, he was still breathing. More than he could say for Lucas Shafer. If Ben had had his back like he was supposed to, Shafer would probably still be breathing, too.

His shoulders and neck tightened, the worry, the guilt, over losing Shafer still raw enough to make him flinch.

Ben rolled his shoulders. Tried that deep-breathing bullshit the shrink had taught him. Thinking about Shafer led to the kinds of aches that Heather had worked out of his muscles the other night with her hands. To the longneck bottles he needed as much as he hated.

To the divorce. And the post-divorce sex a few weeks ago.

At least the girl, at least Carlie, had survived the accident.

Out of the shower, he toweled off and stepped into a pair of sweats. Shot the longneck standing there in front of the round mirror on the wall, barely bigger than a quarter. Steam hung in the air. Ben swiped at the mirror with his towel and then tossed it to the floor. He hadn't shaved in a few days. When he noticed a touch of gray in the scruff on his face, he leaned forward over the sink to examine it closer.

Not quite thirty-five years old, and his facial hair was turning gray. Ben smoothed his hands over his cheeks and dragged them down his face. Son-of-a-bitch. Bags under his eyes, too. He flicked his eyes down over his shoulders and chest and allowed himself a moment of pride, of relief, that he might be aging, but he was in damned good shape. Next, he swept his gaze up to his thick, dark hair. No signs of gray there.

What had Heather said the other night? When she was straddling him on the couch? She had pushed his face between her bare breasts and moaned something about a silver fox. He wasn't a silver fox, was he? Well, no, Ben didn't consider himself a fox in any form or color.

*Pray with me.*

Why did that bother him?

The girl had been terrified, and she had every right to be. Hell, she most likely wasn't out of the woods yet and still had every right to be afraid of dying. Or living—Ben had seen accidents like hers before, and the fear of permanent repercussions wasn't out of the question.

The sound of his phone ringing from the kitchen drew him from his thoughts. Eyes still locked with his own in the mirror, Ben stepped back and turned away. Still in just the dark sweats, he hooked his fingers around the neck of the empty bottle and moseyed out to the kitchen.

He had missed Heather's call by two seconds, tops. Hoping to hear his little girl's voice, he tapped the missed call on the screen and listened to the ringing.

"Hey."

Heather would have worked all day, but she didn't sound harried or worn out. In fact, Ben would almost say she sounded happy to hear from him. That bothered him. Splitting up had been hard. Ben didn't want to string Heather along if she had any thoughts of a permanent reconciliation. Nothing had changed as far as he was concerned. The bottle in his hand was proof of that.

"Hey. How's Naomi?"

"Good."

He could hear Heather moving around the kitchen. Heard pots and pans banging. She was probably going to fix dinner for herself and Naomi. Chicken nuggets. Mac and cheese. A vegetable. Ben hated anything but corn, but Heather insisted their daughter wouldn't be a picky eater.

"What's she doing?"

"Reading a story to her dolls," Heather answered.

"Mmm. Are they all paying attention?"

"Of course." The laugh used to touch him. In fact, just

a week ago, that laugh would have done something to him. "Wanna come for dinner?"

And a week ago, because of that laugh, Ben would have accepted the invitation. Depending on where Naomi was and what she was doing, Ben would have done his best to steal kisses. To cop a feel. Heather turned him on, and selfish jerk that he was, if she was going to let him play with her, he was going to do it.

"No."

He hadn't realized he would turn her down until he heard himself speak.

"No?" Heather sounded shocked. "Why not?"

Ben huffed out a sigh. Why not? What did he have to do? He could go see his little girl. But he had to stay away from Heather. He needed to put just a bit of space between them, because when he was around her, he was greedy, and he was only going to end up hurting her. Which would hurt Naomi in the long run.

"Oh."

"Oh what?" He propped his butt on the tiny counter at his back and crossed his bare feet.

"You have a date?"

"I don't date," he answered simply. "You know that."

Heather hummed in answer.

"I just—"

"Gonna hit up the bar and find someone to take home?"

He hadn't planned to do that, but when Heather suggested it, his dick perked up, ready for action. He could. There was no shortage of bars in town and no shortage of women willing to come home with a guy looking for a night of dirty sex.

Ben squeezed his eyes closed for a second. Hard, dirty sex. Hot slick skin and a raging hard-on and shooting his wad might be just what he needed. For two seconds. But then he'd have a stranger here, and he would have to be an ass and chase her out.

The apartment would be empty again.

He would be left alone with his demons.

Wasn't worth it.

"No." He pushed off the counter and turned to the permanently spotted stainless steel sink to rinse his bottle out. "I'm gonna crash, actually. I'm beat."

"Really?"

"Mmm." He tossed the bottle in the recycle and left the kitchen.

"Were you on scene at that big accident earlier this week? The one on Broadway?"

"Yeah."

"I saw the news. Looked pretty bad."

"Yep." He ground the word out as he entered his bedroom. The drapes were open, but the window was tiny. He hated the gloom in here, too. Maybe this room was worse than the shower.

Actually, the kitchen sucked, too. Seemed like every room where he was sucked, which made him decide it was himself that he couldn't stand. After all, he hadn't like himself much when he lived in the house with Heather and Naomi either.

*No kidding, Sager.*

"You wanna talk about it?" Heather asked softly.

"No."

He hated talking about it—about the horrific things he had seen on the job. He didn't want to relive any of it. He didn't want to parse out details of someone else's tragedies, even if it was simply to move past the trauma himself. How the hell did soldiers manage to come home from war and live again? Jesus, no wonder so many veterans dealt with PTSD.

"Okay. Get some rest, Ben."

"Yeah. Thanks."

He ended the call before Heather could say more. From the foot of his bed, he stared at the pillow for a moment. Outside, a cold rain fell. Wasn't that much warmer in here.

*Pray with me.*

To hell with it. Ben tossed his phone on the bed, stripped out of the sweats, and dressed this time in faded denim, a plain gray fleece, and worn, comfy boots.

He just needed to see for himself that the girl was okay. Maybe if he saw her, if he saw that Aaron was there with her, he could move on to the next crisis.

# CHAPTER
# FIVE

*Six Weeks Later*

S Carlie rubbed absently at the ache in her hip. It was feeling better; everything was feeling better, but she was always sore after a physical therapy appointment. She eyed the Beanstalks menu board behind the counter and wished she had an appetite.

"Can I help you?"

She stepped up to the counter when Rita, the cashier, turned to her. Behind her, the door to the café opened, and a brutal winter wind whipped inside with the latest customer. That didn't help either. Winter, in general, could be hard enough to deal with, but the icy cold and that vicious wind tended to make her legs and her back hurt more.

"I'll take an unsweetened iced tea," she decided, eyes still on the menu board. The pear salad with honey vinaigrette sounded good. But so did the tomato bisque. Carlie shivered when the door opened again, and another gust of wind rustled the fliers on the billboard on the wall to her right.

"Anything else?" Rita asked hopefully. Carlie barely held back a laugh. She was in here often, since the café was just a few doors down from the travel agency, and she used to order food. She had never been one of those girls to pick at a salad and worry about putting on weight. Rita probably thought she'd jumped the good food ship to dive into the carb-watching waters.

"Can I get the honey pear salad and a cup of tomato bisque?" Carlie added to her order.

"Of course!"

Obviously pleased that Carlie had decided to eat, the woman set about getting her order ready. Carlie glanced at her phone while she waited, but when she found nothing new there, she dropped it back in her purse and lifted her head to look around. Two young moms stood together in line behind her—one held a car seat with a fluffy blanket tossed over the top and the other held a little boy. Carlie offered the women a smile when they noticed her looking and then continued her perusal of the familiar café.

A guy stood at the east wall, clearly uncomfortable in the kitschy surroundings. Even in his navy Carhart coat, Carlie could see his shoulders hunched up around his ears. It wasn't often she saw men in here, and if she did, it was usually with a woman, at the counter to order something on the go. The pastel floral décor and the acoustic music wasn't terribly masculine.

Carlie let her eyes slide down over the guy's backside. She was recovering from injuries, not death, after all. He filled out his worn denim and then some; Carlie bit her lip and took another peek at his butt. Very nice. His thighs looked powerful, too. Realizing suddenly that she was staring at a stranger's butt in a public place, she gave herself a mental shake and turned back to the counter.

Rita sent her a quick grin and nodded as if she were agreeing the guy was worth a good, long look. Carlie felt her cheeks twinge with a blush, but she smiled back. Busted, but at least the guy hadn't caught her staring. When Rita gave her a total, she handed her debit card over and then tucked it back inside her purse.

The guy turned as she carried her to-go bag and her tea by him. The bit of scruff on his face and the hard lines of his cheekbones would have caught her eye, anyway, but his eyes stopped her in her tracks. She knew this guy. She knew those electric blue eyes and the thick fringe of lashes that framed them.

"Hey." His voice was scratchy and deep, the way she remembered it, but his lips tipped up in a small smile. Carlie wondered if he remembered her and then told herself not to be ridiculous. It wasn't every day that she was pulled from a totaled vehicle, but this guy surely helped women and men alike, all day every day.

"Hi." She nodded, a smile itching to cut loose on her lips. She kept moving, though, telling herself that pull she felt toward him was hero worship now that she realized he was the first responder who had rescued her the night of the accident.

"Carlie, right?"

She stilled when he spoke her name, embarrassed by the tiny thrill that zinged through her. Ben. She'd found out that the man who pulled her from the wreckage of her SUV was Ben Sager.

Those first days after the accident, in and out of consciousness, Carlie had the strangest dreams. She had heard his voice hundreds of times, the way he had kept her calm when she was trapped in the car, when the pain had been so bad, she couldn't breathe.

And his eyes—

"Yeah." She turned to give him a small smile. "Carlie."

"Hey."

The slow slide and tip of his lips into a sexy grin set flight to butterflies in her belly. Wow. Erin was going to love this. She had talked with Erin about Ben enough that anyone who overheard her might assume she *actually knew* him. Erin would laugh at Carlie bumping into the guy in a café and flipping out when he smiled at her.

*Get over it, Carlie.*

"I'm Ben," he told her, as if she needed the reminder.

"I know." She nodded. She might have said more; Carlie loved to talk. But those butterflies were flapping their wings in her throat now. Or maybe it was her heart beating in her throat. Whatever it was, Carlie found herself tongue tied and breathless.

"How are you?" Hands in his coat pockets, he let his eyes roam down over her navy peacoat and her khakis. Carlie took that opportunity to force herself to breathe. But she was still lightheaded from his attention or his grin or the blue eyes.

"Doing okay," she answered truthfully. "One day at a time."

"Good," he answered with a slow nod. "So." He shrugged and took a deep breath. Carlie thought he looked a little fidgety. "I stopped in to see you in the hospital. Do you remember that?"

"Sort of."

The two young moms behind her in line slipped by now with their orders. Feeling self-conscious under Ben's intense stare, Carlie watched them claim a table across the room.

"Was Aaron there? He showed up for you, right?"

*Erin?*

Carlie whipped her head back around and studied him with narrowed eyes. How did he know Erin?

"Erin?" she asked with a frown.

"You were talking about him at the scene of the accident."

Carlie quirked an eyebrow at Ben and then closed her eyes. She didn't remember that. Talking about Erin. She didn't remember the accident itself and very little of the whole night had come back to her. Mostly, the memory of the pain and the terror she felt when she couldn't move, both from the pressure of the crushed metal pinning her in place and not being able to even wiggle her toes in her shoes.

"I was...I talked about Erin? At the accident?"

Ben glanced at the bag in her hand. "I should let you go."

"Erin's my best friend," Carlie explained. "She and I were supposed to leave..." She cleared her throat, still emotional about the wreck and the scare even after six weeks had passed. "We were supposed to fly to Florida the next day."

"Oh." He flashed her a big grin and laughed softly. "Okay. You were talking about someone named Aaron. I assumed it was a boyfriend."

"Because it was bad." Her whisper was gruff, her throat tight with emotion.

Ben gave her a small shrug and a nod.

"I kept wondering how you were and hoping that he was the kind of guy who would be there for you. Through your recovery."

Carlie pressed her lips together. "Thank you. That means a lot to me."

Ben nodded at the bag in her hand again. "You should eat that before it gets cold."

The soup wasn't going to get cold immediately. Carlie knew it was piping hot when Rita spooned it into the paper cup. She did want to eat, but on the other hand, she was drawn to him. If he was willing to stand there and give her his attention, Carlie wanted to talk to him. Made no sense, but she felt like she knew him. She was attracted to him in ways that had nothing to do with his bedroom eyes or sexy smile.

She had dated some in high school. Fallen for someone in college, though it hadn't lasted. But she wasn't sure she had ever felt that deep, soul-quenching connection she had felt with Ben the night he talked her through the rescue.

*He saved your life, Carlie. You would feel this attraction to him, this yearning to know him, even if he was a bald, pot-bellied grandpa.*

"Wanna join me?" She nodded her head at a two-top table away from the door. As much as she wanted to talk to him longer, she couldn't take the frigid air.

Ben tipped his head, clearly surprised at the invitation. Carlie wasn't shy, and she had always enjoyed people. But something about this guy made her jittery, so she was a little surprised she had asked Ben to sit and even more surprised that her voice sounded normal.

"I do." He nodded. "Are you sure you don't mind?"

"Not at all." She slipped by him and led the way to the table she had her eyes on—across the room, away from the door.

"What do you recommend?" He followed her to the table but looked over his shoulder at the menu board.

She smiled when he sent her a sheepish grin.

"Everything's good," she answered as she slipped her coat off and hung it on her chair. "The chicken sandwich on the top is really good."

"Great." He locked eyes with her and nodded. "I'll be right back."

Carlie sat and reached for her bag. When Rita noticed Ben at the counter, she shot Carlie a quick peek. Carlie laughed when Rita winked and turned back to Ben.

What was this about? Carlie wondered. First, what was Ben Sager doing at the café? She frequented the place and had never seen him here before. Second, what was she thinking, inviting him to join her?

While Ben was at the counter to order, Carlie slipped her phone from her purse and texted Erin.

*Having lunch with Ben.*

Three floating dots appeared on the screen immediately. Carlie peeked at the counter to make sure Ben didn't surprise her and catch her texting about him.

*Ben Who? Ben the fireman? Deets, please.*

"You sure you don't mind sharing your lunch hour with me?"

Carlie felt heat flood her cheeks when she heard Ben's voice close to her again. She swallowed hard and hoped to manage the blush and the ridiculous, sloppy grin when she looked up at him.

"Hundred percent sure," she promised him.

# CHAPTER
# SIX

Ben set his tray on the table and shrugged out of his coat, all the while wondering what the hell he was doing. He had come here looking for a birthday gift for Heather. Places like this made him jumpy; he still had a funky itch between his shoulders.

Carlie watched him drop into the chair across from him. She stared at him boldly when he studied her face, only a touch of pink in her cheeks. Ben decided the color was the cold weather outside and the overly warm interior of the café. Had nothing to do with him. He was sure of that.

"I get the feeling you don't come here often."

He had dropped his gaze to examine the southwestern chicken sandwich she had recommended, but now, he jerked his chin up to look at her again. The smile she wore was more challenging than sweet. Almost flirty.

Which was crazy. A kid like Carlie Beringer wasn't going to flirt with a guy like him. He gave her a small smile and snagged his cup for a drink.

Too bad. He wouldn't mind flirting with the blonde. She checked all the boxes—petite, intriguing brown eyes, and pretty pink lips that apparently loved to smile.

*Kissable.*

*Jesus, Ben. Where did that come from?*

"I don't," he finally found his voice, careful to keep his eyes just over her shoulder. The wall behind her was boring as hell but definitely safer. He sipped his black-berry tea and studied his sandwich again. "I'm looking for a gift."

"Ah." Carlie nodded. While he had ordered, she had taken a salad and a cup of soup from her bag, but now she only fiddled with the plastic silverware. "For your wife?"

Startled by her assumption, Ben jerked his gaze up to meet her eyes again.

"No." He shook his head. She stared at him silently. He could lie. Tell her he was getting something for his sister. But why? They'd bumped into each other accidentally, so maybe this was the universe's way of letting him know she was okay. A quick lunch together and they would head their separate ways.

Or maybe it was the universe's way of telling him she wasn't dating someone named Aaron.

He squirmed in his chair and picked up the sandwich. Carlie blinked and looked at her soup when he took a bite. At least now he could breathe, without her intense stare pinning him in place. He could *think*.

Just because she wasn't dating someone named Aaron didn't mean she was single.

Which didn't matter in the least, he reminded himself.

"Um. Ex-wife, actually," he mumbled after he swallowed.

"Oh." She reached for the cup of soup and dipped her spoon in, but she still didn't take a bite.

"Her birthday's coming up." He wiped his mouth with his napkin and shrugged. "Next week."

Carlie nodded. She glanced at him like she wanted to say something, but instead, she finally tasted her soup.

"Is it good?"

"Hmm?" She quirked an eyebrow at him and then grinned and nodded. "This? Yes. I think everything's good here."

"And do you actually eat the sandwiches?" he asked her skeptically.

"I do." She laughed and sat back in her chair. "I like food."

"Oh, I can tell." Ben eyed her mostly uneaten lunch and then looked back at her with a small smile.

"Well." She huffed out a sigh. "I do. But I haven't had much of an appetite since the accident."

"Oh."

"I still don't remember much," she said softly.

"That might be a good thing."

She cleared her throat and stared at him for a moment. "Maybe. I do remember..."

Little red dots sat on her cheeks now like dimes. Ben watched her patiently, wondering what she was thinking.

"You being there." She shrugged and shook her head. "I remember you talking to me. Trying to keep me calm."

"I hope it helped. Knowing we were there."

Their eyes met and held, but Carlie jerked her face away when her eyes filled. She nodded and blinked furiously, only looking back at him when she was in control again.

"So." She cleared her throat again. "What sorts of things does your ex-wife like?"

Ben groaned and looked around the overly feminine café. The floral décor made him want to climb the walls. Thank God Heather hadn't decorated their house like this.

"Um. Flowers. Plants. Pillows." He waved his hand absently. "Girly stuff."

Carlie snorted and rolled her eyes. "So, you're the kind of guy who breaks out in hives when surrounded by girly things? Let me guess. You don't own a stitch of pink clothing."

"Bingo."

"Does she like incense? Or essential oils?"

"No. She won't use any of that stuff because of Naomi's asthma."

Ben expected Carlie to ask about Naomi, but she looked around again, as if shopping from her seat.

"What about a journal? Or a daily devotional book?"

Heather might like something like that, but the thought made Ben break out in a cold sweat.

"Maybe," he admitted.

"Oh! I know! What about one of those painted wine glasses? They're so cute!"

"She doesn't drink wine."

"Mmm." Carlie nodded. "Okay. Coffee? They have a really cute line of coffee mugs, too."

Ben's soft laugh drew Carlie's attention away from the wares the café offered and back to him.

"What?" She bit her lip as an innocent grin spread over her face.

"Why do women get so excited over painted coffee mugs and wine glasses and water bottles?"

Carlie laughed and shrugged as she reached for her cup.

"I don't know." She took a drink, set the cup down, and reached to tuck a lock of hair behind her ear. "Pretty water bottles make it more fun to drink water."

Ben tipped his head with a frown. "But...why does drinking water have to be fun?"

"Well. I mean." Carlie stared at him, seemingly a little bit frazzled and a little bit amused. "It's important to drink a lot of water, right? But it's boring. So. If you jazz up your cup or your bottle, it's more fun."

Ben narrowed his eyes at her in thought. When Carlie stared back at him boldly, he finally shrugged and nodded. Heather might not have said that in so many words, but it seemed like she had said something to that effect.

"Fair enough."

"So." Carlie raised her eyebrows. Ben's heart slammed against his ribs when she wet her lips with the tip of her tongue. She said something else, but still caught up on that flash of pink, Ben missed it. He stared at her silently and nearly swallowed his own tongue when she asked what he thought.

"I'm sorry." He gave himself a mental shake. "I wasn't listening."

Eyes locked with his, Carlie stared at him for a moment before speaking again. "I said, if your ex-wife drinks water, they do have a cute line of fancy water bottles, too."

"Of course, they do," he said with a soft laugh. "What about you?"

"Well, we've established that I like cute wine glasses, coffee mugs, and water bottles. So, I'm not sure what you're asking me."

*Shit. Busted.*

He had no idea what he was asking, either, but he was desperate for her to say it, *to talk about herself.* Hell, he hadn't felt this keyed up over anything since Bozeman got that new pickup truck. Hadn't been this amped up over a woman since he'd asked Heather to go to a football game with him in high school.

"When's your birthday?"

No idea where that question had come from, but he was curious.

"September."

"Hmm." He nodded.

"For the record, my favorite color is green, and I love that coffee mug up there."

They shared a smile that lingered for a long moment before he turned to look at the coffee mug she liked.

"The bright green one?"

"Kelly green," she said and nodded when he looked back at her.

"Okay, well, if I'm going to deliver, I'm gonna need to know how to get a hold of you."

*Shit. Did he just ask her for her phone number?*

He wanted her number. Hell yes, he wanted Carlie Beringer's number. But he felt kind of weird asking for it. She was ten years younger than him. She'd been in a bad situation when they met, vulnerable and desperate. Was asking for her number now a violation?

"Give me your phone." She held out her hand, taking his phone when he pulled it from his coat pocket and handed it over to her. Ben held his breath for a second while she studied his lock screen photo. "Is this Naomi?"

He nodded.

"How old is she?"

"Three."

"God, she's adorable," Carlie told him. "Love her face."

The picture was of Naomi in a red parka, white fur-trimmed hood up over her head. Her big smile bunched her cheeks up like apples and almost hid her eyes.

"Six four three nine."

"What?" She frowned and cut a glance at him without lifting her head.

"The code for my phone." He nodded at the smart-phone in her hand.

"Oh." She tapped it in and then tapped his contact icon. Ben's mouth went dry as she tapped at the screen. Finally, she handed it back to him. "Okay. Message me so I know it's you."

"And what if I want to surprise you?"

Carlie opened her mouth to answer him, eyes a bit dazed looking. Instead, she bit her lip again and finally laughed and drew a quick breath.

"Oh, you did," she assured him.

He wondered what that meant, but rather than ask— it seemed like a good thing, but he wasn't going to fish for compliments or proof of flirting, thank you very much —he tapped out a quick hi to her. Her eyes lit up when they heard the muted ding of her phone.

"I think it's only fair that I get to see your lock screen."

He had no idea where those words had come from, but again, he liked the idea and suddenly, he very much wanted to see the lock screen of her phone.

"Oh." She swallowed hard and ducked her head as she fished her phone from her purse. Ben wasn't positive, but it looked like a rush of color had touched her cheeks again. Why would that be? Did she have a picture of an ex as her lock screen? Or worse? Did she have a picture of herself and a boyfriend she hadn't mentioned?

*You didn't ask, Sager.*

She handed the phone over the table. Ben made sure to rub his finger over hers when he took it, but he wasn't prepared for the zing that ripped from his finger to his heart to his groin. Carlie's eyes flashed, making him wonder if she felt it too.

He stared at her face for a moment, marking her pert little nose. The two freckles on the bridge of her nose. The moon shaped scar on her forehead. The dimple at the corner of her lips.

His eyes dropped to her throat when she gulped and swallowed hard.

"What?" she whispered.

Ben only shook his head and turned his attention to her phone. The picture was a sunrise shot. The light climbing, elbowing its way up over the ocean. A bit of foam at the shoreline. Driftwood. A pair of green flip flops.

"Where's this?" he asked, genuinely interested. He pictured her somewhere on that beach. Kicked back on a lounge chair. Skimpy cut off shorts. A green bikini top. Maybe a straw hat protecting her fair skin. Nothing but the sound of waves and her sweet laughter.

"Destin."

"Nice."

A text dropped as he studied the picture. He jerked, ready to hand the phone over to her, but his name caught his eye. His name? Why would someone be texting about him?

*Carlie. Seriously. You've had sex faster than lunch with Ben. Dying for details.*

Heart pounding out of his chest and dick trying to pound out of the blue jeans he'd pulled on earlier, he pretended he hadn't seen the message—She'd told Erin that she was having lunch with him?—and handed the phone back to her.

*Sex.*

Dammit all. He'd been tiptoeing up to that in his head, but Carlie's friend had yanked him right up nose to nose with the thought of Carlie and sex.

God, he wanted to drag the woman over the table

and settle her right down on his lap. Nope. He'd stand. Lay her back over the table and pound his cock inside her. Hell, they'd rock the table off its legs. Knock over the whole damned building.

"Erin and I were supposed to go back," she said quietly, completely unaware that Ben's brain had turned to the neanderthal level of a teen boy's, and he was mentally pounding her on the café table.

"You'll get to go again," he assured her.

"We're supposed to go to South Carolina next." Her smile touched something else inside him. Higher than his cock. Just above his belly. She looked both content and hopeful at the same time. He wished he was the reason for the look.

Maybe he wouldn't lay her down and ride her hard and fast. Maybe he would rather unwrap her and cherish her like a gift. Trail kisses from her forehead down over her lips and her belly to the heat between her legs.

*Jesus, Sager.*

"I should get back to work," she announced.

He nodded and watched her stand to put her coat on. He would give it a minute, let her leave before standing. Either that or advertise to her and the rest of the female population here that he had a hard-on for her.

"Are you gonna call me?" she asked as she pulled her purse over her shoulder and tucked her hands in her pockets.

"Do you want me to call you, Carlie Beringer?"

She tugged on her lip with her teeth and stole Ben's breath away again.

"Yeah. I do."

# CHAPTER
# SEVEN

Her trip to Greece had been the adventure of a lifetime. Carlie had been a little anxious when she went, traveling such a distance alone. But the sea and the coastline had mesmerized her, and the people she met had been so warm and welcoming, she had been tempted once or twice not to come home. The memories tugged at her heart now and made her a little blue. She needed to finish putting together the travel itinerary for Ginger and Maury Garman, so she had no time to ruminate over memories and the fact that other than her dog and her best friend, she had no one to share them with.

She stilled her fingers over her keyboard now and dropped her head back to take a deep breath. Since the accident, she had spent a lot of evenings alone dwelling on the fact that she was *alone*. And now, those maudlin thoughts were creeping into her workdays, too. Erin had suggested she might need to see a therapist. Carlie took another deep breath, irritated with herself and restless because she was irritated. She hadn't died in the damned accident.

And this was the hell of it—she didn't remember much about the accident. But from what she had been told—both from her parents and the police—it could have been fatal. Her life could have ended at twenty-five. And she had nothing to show for it.

That wasn't true, and she knew it. She loved the little house she shared with her dog. Decorated with bright colored pillows and curtains, fun artwork, and piles of books, it was the perfect reflection of who she was. She had the unconditional love of a dog, and Nash meant everything to her. And she had a job she loved, whether it was traveling and sharing her experiences with her clients or planning the perfect trip for someone else.

But she didn't have love. She didn't have a special someone. And now, she could have died, and only her dog would have been at home to miss her.

Okay, that was a bit much. Carlie rolled her eyes. Her parents and her brother would miss her. But that wasn't the point, either. She wanted someone to love. Her parents had been happily married for thirty-one years, and her brother and his wife were happy. Carlie loved romance books and rom-com movies. She absolutely believed in love, in everyone having a soulmate out there in the world.

She had a better chance than a lot of people to find her soulmate somewhere in the world since she traveled as much as she did. But one thing she didn't have was patience. And now, after the accident, after facing life-threatening injuries and dealing with a long physical recovery, instead of feeling Zenlike and at peace, she was in even more of a hurry to get on with her life.

With the good stuff.

Her phone buzzed on her desk. Remembering that Ben Sager had her number now, she nearly lunged for it, moving so quickly, her chair almost shot out from under her. She swallowed hard and reminded herself that just because Ben had her number didn't mean he was going to call or text. This text was from Erin.

*Drinks after work?*

They hadn't gone out for a while, and if she were being honest, she wanted to see Erin. To gush about Ben.

Maybe if she shared with her bestie how Ben had spoken to her, how he had recognized her, the buzz of excitement in her belly would fade away. Maybe hearing her voice say the crazy things she was thinking about Ben Sager would make her silly crush go away.

She sent Erin a yes and then gave herself a mental shake and forced herself to get busy. The sooner she finished the itinerary for the Garmans the sooner she could head out to meet Erin. She wasn't ready to indulge herself with a margarita—the trauma from the accident was still too fresh, and she hadn't even been drinking that night. But maybe she could drink a light beer and munch on something and feel okay to drive home.

Carlie met Erin at Jameson's—a neighborhood pub two blocks from her place and two blocks the other way from Erin's. Carlie's SUV had been totaled, so she parked the new-to-her compact car at the curb just behind Erin. The wind had been blustery and cruel all day, so she took a moment to bundle up before stepping out. Coat zipped and scarf wrapped around her neck, she pulled in a deep breath and opened the door to brave the elements.

The memory of the sweet little face surrounded by the fake white fur and a red parka hood hit her as she swung her door closed. Naomi. Carlie hadn't asked, but she had to assume the little girl was Ben's daughter. She had his eyes. As Carlie made her way to the door of the bar, she wondered about the first responder and his ex-wife.

Why were they divorced? Did he see his little girl often? How long had they been divorced? How did they know Naomi had asthma? Did the little girl have an attack?

When she pulled the door open to step inside, Carlie was wondering if Naomi had ever had breathing treatments or if she had ever been rushed to the ER. As if it was any of her business. She was glad for the dimly lit bar when she felt the rush of heat in her face. Daydreaming about this guy like anything about him was her business, when in fact, she knew next to nothing about him and probably would never hear from him again.

Erin called her a hopeless romantic, but even Erin would roll her eyes at her musings about Ben's daughter. Carlie's brother rolled his eyes at her all the time, and even her mom called her a dreamer. Carlie countered with the fact that she had apparently been raised in a house full of love since she was so adamant to find it for herself.

The tension in her shoulders unwound when she saw Erin at a high-top table with a basket of chips and a pint glass in front of her. Erin's enthusiastic wave threw Carlie's reserve about Ben and his daughter out the window. She would at least gush to Erin about the smokin' hot first responder who had pulled her from the wreckage and sent her into dreamland with those bedroom eyes.

# EIGHT

"But he remembered you," Erin countered yet again.

"Remembering that he cut my car open with a giant can opener to pull me out doesn't mean anything, Erin."

She wished it did. But she was good at getting her hopes up, romanticizing things, on her own. While part of her loved Erin for playing along with her crush that might just be a little bit of hero worship or misplaced gratitude, most of her regretted telling Erin about bumping into Ben at the café.

As much fun as it was to obsess about Ben Sager with moony eyes and dreamy sighs, it wasn't realistic, and Carlie needed to get her feet on the ground and her head out of the clouds. The physical repercussions of the accident had been bad enough. She couldn't afford to lose herself in a crazy, pointless crush on a man who probably hadn't thought twice about her until seeing her today.

Erin drained her second beer and shrugged.

"Okay, so how about online dating? My coworker was talking about some new dating app."

"No."

"Why not?"

"Not interested." Carlie shrugged as she fiddled with her empty bottle.

"Okay." Erin held her hands up in surrender.

"What about you?" Carlie arched an eyebrow at her. "What's going on with Matthew?"

Carlie couldn't help the laughter when Erin rolled her eyes. Matthew Koonz, another of Erin's coworkers, had been asking her out now for at least a year. Carlie had met him—the guy was a hot mess, but good friend material.

Erin nibbled on her lower lip.

"What?" Carlie nearly launched herself over the table. Pain shot up her through her lower back at the sudden movement, but she schooled her features so Erin wouldn't notice. "What's going on?" Instead of excitedly pouncing on her friend, Carlie simply reached over the table and touched the back of Erin's hand.

"I signed up." Erin licked her lips. "On the app."

"Yeah? Find anyone you'd swipe right for?"

"Lots of gorgeous pictures," Erin said with a nod. "But I'm sure at least half of them aren't real."

"Matthew said he would take you out on his grandpa's boat."

"It's a Jon boat, Carlie." Erin tilted her head. "Something tells me I'd have a fishing pole in hand and a bucket of live bait at my feet."

"He has a cute dimple."

Erin nodded begrudgingly. "Not my dream guy," she mumbled. "I mean, here you are, with a dreamy guy in sights, and you're sitting here at Jameson's with me."

Carlie grinned and slid off the chair with caution. Erin was watching her when she looked back at her.

"Perfectly happy to be stuck with you," she announced. "I gotta get home to Nash."

Erin stood, too, and hugged her goodbye.

"Goodnight, Carlie."

BRICKED AND VINYL-SIDED bungalows lined both sides of the street on her short drive home. Maybe she was feeling a little lonely, but she was a happy person. She didn't want to let her accident take that from her. If anything, she decided as she pulled to a stop at the curb in front of the house she rented, she needed to wake up and live for the now. Enjoy every moment and stop worrying so much about the future.

Nash met her at the door as she stepped inside. Carlie tossed her purse and keys on the table just inside the door and leaned over to hug him. If she were going to start counting blessings, Nash would be at the top of the list.

"Hi buddy," she crooned as she scratched his ears and dropped a kiss on his head. "Wanna go outside?"

The bark and tail wag as he slipped past her and ran to the door made her laugh. Carlie snagged the leash off the hook by the door, clipped it to Nash's collar, and stepped back out into the brisk winter air.

Outside, a winter hush had fallen over the street. Carlie stood in her tiny yard and tapped her feet to keep warm while Nash did his business.

She was worried that Erin had jumped into the online dating world. Carlie believed everyone deserved happiness, but she wasn't convinced technology had a place in romance.

That thought brought her right back to Ben. And his ex-wife.

*Why were they divorced?*

As much as Carlie believed in true love, she understood that not every relationship was made to last. But damned if she wasn't curious about Ben and his ex.

Nash, business done, and excess energy burned off from running back and forth in the yard, trotted back to Carlie to sit at her feet. After one last look around—the sky was overcast, no stars in sight—Carlie hurried back to the house and let Nash off the leash as she closed the door behind her.

He zoomed through the house, either looking for water or his stuffed dinosaur, as Carlie toed her shoes off, shrugged out of her coat, and carried it to her room where she tossed it over her bed before going to the kitchen to get Nash water.

Dark had fallen as she was leaving work, and she had spent a couple of hours catching up with Erin. But it was still early. She could sit down with a book or turn on a movie. Still hungry after eating only the chips and salsa at the bar, she dug around in the refrigerator and pulled out a container of leftover soup.

Perfect.

Once she reheated it on the stovetop, she carried a bowl to the little living area and almost sat down. She remembered her phone, though, and plucked it out of her purse. Finding the TV remote on the couch, she picked it up and turned the TV on.

Reruns of *The Golden Girls*.

Perfect, she decided.

Nash trotted in with his toy dinosaur in his mouth. He hopped up to sit beside her. Carlie scratched his neck and then turned her attention to her soup. Eyes on the TV, she laughed at Blanche and Rose. Blanche was her favorite of the girls, but she figured people would assume she liked Rose best. Some people would probably compare her to Rose.

Their mistake.

She wasn't naïve. Just a hopeless romantic.

When her phone buzzed against her thigh, Carlie groped for it and picked it up, expecting a text from Erin. Maybe she had found someone interesting on the dating app.

When *The Golden Girls* went to commercial, Carlie finally looked at her phone.

*She loved the water bottle.*

There had been women since Heather. Girls before Heather. Ben Sager knew what he was doing with a woman's body. He played Heather's like a master guitarist. Before he started dating Heather, girls flocked to him, and those that he did go out with her were eager to please and even easier to please.

But that didn't mean he *understood* women. Obviously. The only woman who had ever wanted to take more from him than what money he had to offer and the orgasms he delivered was now his ex-wife.

He stared at his phone, waiting, hoping to see the three dots that would indicate Carlie was going to answer.

What the hell was he doing? If Heather deserved better than to be saddled with him, then this kid sure as hell deserved better. So what if she had been friendly? They shared a table for lunch. End of story.

Well. Not, though. Carlie had given him her number. Maybe she'd done it thinking he wouldn't use it. But then again, she had told him she wanted him to contact her.

Still, totally possible she was playing games with him, right?

*The water bottle? I thought you would go for the coffee mug.*

Ben fought off the stupid grin when Carlie's text dropped on his phone.

*She uses a world's best mom cup from Naomi.*

*Do you?*

*Do I what?*

*Use a world's best dad cup from Naomi?*

Ben held his breath for a second. He hadn't spelled it out for Carlie that Naomi was his daughter, but it was obvious.

He wondered what Carlie thought of that. Hell, three strikes against him right there—older, divorced, and a part-time dad, thanks to his job and the custody agreement. Feet propped on his IKEA coffee table, Ben dropped his head back to rest on the couch he'd brought with him from his and Heather's basement. His phone, still in his hand, buzzed again.

*I assume Naomi is your daughter. Am I wrong?*

He answered her immediately. Not because he worried about what she would think. But because he had regretted every second of the day since bumping into her at Beanstalks that he didn't gush to her about his little girl.

*She's my little girl. And yes, I do have a world's best dad coffee cup.*

*Are you, though? Because my dad's pretty freaking cool.*

*What's your dad bench?*

This time the buzzing was continuous. Ben stared at her name and number on his screen for half a second before answering.

"Hey."

A sweet, hearty laugh greeted him.

"Seriously? *What does my dad bench?*"

"Well, I mean you make claims. You gotta back 'em up."

"That's priceless," she announced. "I don't know what Dad benches these days. I'll have to ask him."

"Don't do that," Ben said quickly. No need to get her dad involved, for Christ's sake. "Just tell me why he's cool."

"Because he makes the best chocolate chip pancakes and mimosas in the world."

"The whole world?" Ben grinned. The threat of Carlie talking to her parents about him gone, the tension in his shoulders and neck eased. He stared at the open long-neck on the table next to his right leg, but he made no move to pick it up. "How do I know you're qualified to make that claim?"

"He makes them for every holiday. The second Sunday of every month. And my birthday."

"Yeah, but the *whole* world?"

"I travel a lot, Ben. Of all the places I've been, no pancakes or mimosas measure up."

"What's his secret?"

"Made with love, of course."

"Hmm." Ben pursed his lips and closed his eyes.

"Hmm what?"

"Well, I mean, I'm betting I bench more than your dad, and I make a damned good chocolate chip pancake —in the shape of a princess, I might add. So, I'm still not convinced."

Carlie's rich laughter warmed him from the inside out.

"What're you doing?" he asked her. Teasing with her was fun, but he was ready to move the conversation away from her dad. Besides, he wanted to know exactly what she was doing so he could picture it.

"Just took my dog out, and now I'm eating soup and watching TV."

"What kinda soup?"

"Leftover cream of turkey and wild rice."

"Did your dad make it?"

That laugh again. Ben had a flash of the mangled metal wreckage. The scared, pale face and the wild eyes looking back at him.

"No. It's from the market."

"And what's on TV?"

"*The Golden Girls.*"

"You watch that, too?"

"You're a fan?" She giggled.

"Heather is," he answered. "My ex. She loves Sophia. Her grandmother was a lot like her."

"I like Blanche," Carlie told him.

"Hmm. Well, you remind me of Rose."

"What're you doing?" she asked him.

"I am kicked back on my couch looking at the TV. But I never turned it on. Too tired to get up and find the remote."

"How long have you been a firefighter?" That question took him by surprise. He eyed the longneck for a moment before shifting his gaze back to the blank TV screen.

"Seventeen years."

"And how many other accident victims that you rescued have you kept in touch with?"

"You gave me your number," he reminded her.

"I did," she agreed. "And I'm glad you used it."

Ben sighed and closed his eyes again. She had wanted him to contact her. What if she was as interested in him as he was in her?

*You're playing with fire, Ben Sager, and you know how fucking stupid that is.*

"Carlie."

Worried that his gruff voice might give away his yearning for her, he cleared his throat.

"Hmm?"

"Sleep well."

# TEN

C arlie heard his voice in her dreams. She'd been hearing it since the accident, but last night was different. Talking with him over the phone had been a little bit fun and flirty. Until he'd ground out her name, almost like he found it painful to say it, and then told her to sleep well.

She hadn't slept well. She'd lain awake far too long thinking about him. He was attracted to her; she had no doubt about that now. The question was where did they go from here?

On the surface, her dreams were tame. Sitting with him on a comfortable sofa in a neutral dreamlike room. Talking. Laughing. In the background, the TV had played music videos, though she couldn't remember a time in her life when she'd ever *watched* a music video. Both fully clothed, room for his ex-wife and daughter between them, nothing had happened in the dream. Not even their elbows or fingers had bumped or touched.

But when she finally dragged herself out of bed this morning and climbed into the shower, the dream had come back to her and left her restless with desire. He had said her name—in the dream—in that same gruff, edgy voice, and she had been fascinated with his lips.

Just a taste. She wanted a taste of his lips, of his tongue—

It was the daydreaming in the shower that left her completely unglued, and now, hours later, talking to a woman on the phone and looking up cruise line protocol regarding the virus and vaccine—Carlie had it all memorized by now, but she was diligent in her responsibilities —her mind kept flashing her bits of the dream and the thoughts that were steamier than her shower. Her hands trembled from time to time as she typed.

Would he text her again? Call her? Calling him last night had been spontaneous and fun—who the hell flirted with a woman by asking what her dad could bench press? And yet, Ben had rolled with it, and she loved talking to him. Hated having to end the call.

At noon, when she walked over to Beanstalks hoping that he might decide to show up there again, she was disappointed. Three older women shared a corner table, a hipster dude stared at a laptop as he sipped his chai tea at the bar, and a young couple shared a sandwich at a table near the door.

No Ben.

She could text him, but she decided against it. It wasn't that she thought women couldn't be the one to pursue a relationship—

*Relationship?*

Standing in line, she ducked her head and waited out the blush. Ben Sager might be interested in her. He might be attracted to her. But she had to be honest with herself. If anything ever happened between them, she knew it would be a short-lived fling. A man like Ben would get bored with her and move on quickly.

Carlie took a salad back to work and parked in the break room. Adrenaline spiked when her phone buzzed. She held her breath when she peeked at it and slumped with disappointment when she saw Erin's name. A pang of guilt hit her hard as she read her friend's text.

She was hoping to hear from Ben.

*Human resources director at Shively Manufacturing wants me 2 meet him 4 coffee tomorrow morning.*

*Y wouldn't he be working tomorrow morning?*

*Dunno. But he's hot.*

*Scale of 1-10.*

*George Clooney.*

"Hmm." Carlie arched her brows and considered Erin on a coffee date with a George-Clooney-level hot guy. A morning coffee date sounded innocent. Maybe even boring. But it didn't seem likely that Erin would have to worry about him kidnapping her and whisking her away to a remote shack to keep her prisoner. Too many people around to witness that on a coffee date.

*I think you should go.*

*Really?*

Before Carlie could text an answer, another text bubble filled her screen. Heat surged through her chest, down her arms, and into her fingertips when she saw Ben's name.

*How did you sleep?*

Heart in her throat, his gruff, sexy voice in her head again, Carlie took a quick breath and flexed her fingers.

*I didn't sleep much.*

*Why not?*

She might be okay with flirting and testing the waters with him. But she wasn't ready to admit to him that she had lain awake thinking about him, remembering the way he said her name before they got off the phone. Instead of telling him the truth, she sent him the shrugging emoji in response.

*Were you able to eat today?*

Carlie stared at his text for a moment, remembering that she had told him she had struggled with her appetite since the accident.

Another text from Erin, but Carlie ignored it for now.

*Eating a salad now.*

*At Beanstalks?*

*Break room. No nice guys to talk to at Beanstalks today.*

Her phone lit up and buzzed with an incoming call, making her belly flip-flop with nerves.

"Hey." She swallowed hard, hoping she didn't sound as stiff as she felt.

"I'm not a nice guy," he said by way of greeting. "You need to know that right now."

Her heart jumped at his words, at the low growl. She believed he was, but then she didn't know him well enough to make that call, did she? She fiddled with her fork for a moment, finally scooped up a slice of boiled egg, and decided to go for lighthearted again.

At least until she had her footing.

"Is that your way of making me say no *hot* guys to talk to at Beanstalks today?"

Ben barked a harsh laugh on the other end of the phone.

"I'm on shift," he told her.

"Gotcha."

"Why didn't you sleep?"

Carlie turned her face away from her phone for a second, a bit stunned by his bold question.

"Thinking," she mumbled.

"Hmm." The quiet murmur sounded like agreement, but she wasn't sure. "Me too."

Carlie pulled her phone away now to look at it in disbelief. What did that mean? Had he been thinking about her? Or just overthinking in general?

"Ben—"

The peel of an alarm—the emergency kind—cut her off.

"Gotta go."

He hung up before she could say a word. Carlie stared at her phone silently. What would she have said to him if there had been time?

*Be careful.* She probably would have said something mindless and mind-numbing, like be careful. Something told her Ben would have laughed at her had she said it, and not in a kind way, either.

*I'm not a nice guy.*

She'd have to come up with something better to say

if they were ever in this situation again—Ben cutting a call short and charging out of the fire station to go running into a burning building. And Carlie left holding a dead phone, dread swallowing her whole.

What if he didn't walk out of that burning building?

# CHAPTER
# ELEVEN

The apartment building currently in flames was vacant. Ben allowed himself a tiny slice of relief, but he immediately squared his shoulders as he took in the scene before him. The structure was sandwiched between residential buildings, and even with those apartments evacuated for the fire, they still had a hell of a job to do here. A thick blanket of dark smoke pressed low over the block, flames raged and licked out the windows and up the brick walls—two of three stories currently engulfed. The adrenaline rush made him want to charge in unprepared, but wisdom had come with age and experience. Far better to await command and follow the standard operating procedure. Hell, good men died even when everyone followed procedure to the letter—look at Shafer. No way Ben would consider putting anyone in his crew in danger.

When their water line was established, Ben and Bozeman headed toward the burning building, axes in hand, with the intent of breaking out the remaining windows for ventilation. Fisher and Forsythe moved to the back of the building with the same intention, as the aerial ladder was raised to the roof. No skylight in this particular building to help with ventilation, so they would cut holes in the roof, check the conditions, and get the hell off the roof as soon as possible.

A second engine arrived as Ben and Bozeman swung their axes, sending broken glass flying. The ventilation would help visibility for the crew, not to mention help any victims who might be squatting illegally in the building.

Once the windows and doors were cleared, Ben and Bozeman made a thorough but quick search of the main floor to be certain no one was trapped. Finding nothing, they climbed to the second floor. Relieved no one was in the building, they escaped the smoke-filled building as members of the truck company moved slowly toward the building, sweeping the hose back and forth, aiming at the base of the fire.

After losing Shafer, Ben found it a struggle to concentrate on scenes like this. Flashbacks plagued him. The moment he had known Shafer was down and not coming out of the fire on his own two feet. The steady beep of the monitor in Shafer's hospital room. Hell, even the ride to the scene—the house fully involved when they got there. The chatter as they pulled their turn-out gear on and psyched themselves up to go at the flames.

Shafer's wife and kids.

How he hadn't killed himself and others in the truck company was beyond him. He shouldn't have been working. He shouldn't have argued when his lieutenant called him out and directed him to do grief counseling. He shouldn't have turned to the bottle and shunned his wife.

He felt different now. Shafer, *losing Shafer*, was still in his heart. But not his head. Ben was focused on the flames, the hose, the water supply. Here and now. The adrenaline rush would cause a crash later, but then he was used to that. They were all used to that.

For now, he was relieved to feel like he belonged on the scene, that he was contributing instead of taking up oxygen and getting in the way.

HE LINGERED IN THE SHOWER, because old habits die hard. And because the hot water felt good on the sore muscles —the ones that hurt when he taxed them, even when he was in perfect physical shape.

Times like these—after walking into a residential fire —he couldn't help but think about Schafer. His crew had essentially put out that fire, but fire can be a cruel bitch. Ben had made the mistake of turning his back for a second, and a tiny smolder left unchecked had stretched and climbed and raced up the western wall of the living room. Schafer yelled and went at the flame; Ben watched as the staircase tumbled down and crushed him. On his hands and knees, Ben assessed his friend, his brother. Knocked unconscious, he was unable to help Ben at all.

Digging and shoving, even kicking at the heavy wooden beams, had been torturous. Too much for one man, and finally Bozeman and James had joined him.

Together, they had finally pulled Schafer free of the weight, but the blow to his back had broken ribs and punctured his lungs. In the days Schafer had laid in the hospital alive only with the help of a machine, Ben had only gone to see him once. And that had been after hours —he'd snuck in and sat with Schafer for what felt like hours, both because of his guilt for his injuries and because he was tempted to leave any time he heard a noise outside the small, sterile hospital room. He didn't want to be seen here. Not after failing his partner.

He thought about Heather, too. Well, he used to. In the beginning of his career, after a day like today, he would stand in the shower and relive the fire. Let the soap and the steam wash it all away. And then he would think about his girlfriend, later his wife, starting with how she cared for him at the sidelines. Cooking. Keeping the house in shape. Washing his clothes. All the things she didn't have time for, since she worked, too. He thought about Heather and the way she loved him, and his body used to come alive with those thoughts.

When Naomi came along, he'd moved away from the dirty thoughts about his wife. For a while, at least. Nothing like the pure, innocent love of a child to remind you of the good in the world.

Though, Ben had still loved thinking about his wife.

And then, eventually, it was Heather and a beer. Just one. Until it became a six pack and Heather. Sometimes a twelve pack and maybe Heather.

Backing under the hot water—he figured he had another five minutes before it turned cold—Ben dashed the water from his eyes and tipped his head down to look at his limp dick. Only when his drinking had been at the worst did thoughts of a naked Heather not turn him on.

Hell, just six weeks ago, they'd torn up the sheets at her house again. He swallowed back the mouthful of guilt now. After all, he had tried to stop her, to stop what they were doing. Reminded her they could end up hurting Naomi. Heather had laughed at him and nipped at his lips and then his neck and his nipples. Somewhere near his hips, she told him she knew given the choice, he would still pick a bottle over her. And then she'd scaled back up his body and impaled herself on him and ridden him so hard and fast, she'd come before he ever felt his balls tighten, ready to explode inside her.

Still nothing.

Ben nudged his dick with a tired sigh. He was exhausted. Now that the water sluicing over his shoulders was lukewarm, his body ached again. He needed sleep. Lots of it. Ignoring that weird, sinking feeling—Jesus, was he so old, he couldn't get it up now? That rarely happened, and he hated the fuck out of the idea of it being a new problem—he shut the water off, reached for his towel, and scrubbed it over his hair. He considered a beer as he toweled off the rest of his body.

It didn't even sound good. He had no desire to guzzle one beer, let alone a couple. No mood to sit and watch mindless TV. While he would love to see Naomi, he had no sudden urge to dress and rush over to Heather's, either.

Alone in his place, drapes drawn, Ben tossed his towel over the shower rod and padded naked to the kitchen. He downed a couple of aspirin, chased it with water, and turned the light off. He brushed his teeth, grabbed his phone, and clutched it in his hand as he crawled into bed.

He dozed off, but when he turned over, he dropped his phone and woke when it thumped on the floor.

"Shit."

He groped for it in the dark and stretched to reach the charger on his garage sale nightstand. The screen lit up when he plugged the charger in. There was a text from Carlie waiting for him.

It had come in hours ago. Maybe while he was in that vacant apartment with those wicked flames.

*I'm not all that into nice guys.*

# CHAPTER
# TWELVE

C arlie checked her phone several times last night after sending that last text. Hoping for a response, yes, since her text was a little incendiary. Risky. She had put herself out there, taken a chance again, and let him know without spelling it out in all caps, that she was interested.

At the very least, she had hoped to get a text from him just to know he was okay.

She'd watched the late news last night, Nash's head in her lap, with bated breath. They'd done a small story on the residential fire, and Carlie had nearly jumped off the couch and crawled into the TV looking for him. She didn't know which station house he worked at—the city had three currently operating and a fourth shut down because of the supposed financial burden its operation put on the town.

On the other hand, it was the only fire reported on the news, so she assumed Ben was there somewhere.

There had been no text last night before she went to bed, and only a text from Erin this morning.

Her workday had been slower; with the lack of client interaction, she had spent the day updating files and doing a little searching of her own for future trip ideas. It had been a while since she'd shared any travel stories on the agency's blog. No one had pushed her about it; after all, she'd been laid up with serious injuries for a long time. She wasn't in any shape to drive a half hour to the next town over for a change of scenery for dinner let alone hop a plane and jet off to Seattle or Hawaii or Punta Cana.

Erin called just before closing time. Again, Carlie had to dash that little jolt of hope that it was Ben. She shouldn't be disappointed to talk to her best friend. She shouldn't wish to talk to a guy over her best friend. Especially a guy who couldn't find the time to let her know he was okay after fighting what looked to her like a hellacious fire.

"Hey!" Carlie put Erin on speaker phone. Her coworkers were all gone, except for Sandy. The older woman knew Erin—in fact, she often referred to Carlie and Erin as the Bobbsey Twins. Might have been okay back when they were much younger, but these days, it spoke to the fact that neither of them was involved in any serious, adult relationship.

"Hi. Got a minute?" Erin sounded out of breath.

"First tell me what you're doing. You sound...busy."

"Gross." Erin's familiar snort sounded through the speaker. "I'm on the stepper."

"Eww." Carlie flinched.

"I'll second that," Sandy called as she stood up from her desk and carried her coffee mug to the break room.

"Hi Sandy!"

"Sandy says hi," Carlie lied. "So? How'd it go?"

"It was…interesting."

"Interesting? What does that mean?"

Carlie tapped a few keys and rolled her head on her shoulders. She was stiff. The day after a PT appointment usually meant some old aches and pains were back to haunt her, but right now she was simply stiff from sitting at her desk for so long.

"I dunno. I liked him?"

"Are you asking me?" Carlie quirked a brow in the direction of her phone.

"He's different, Carlie."

"Different, like he doesn't look like George Clooney after all?"

"No, he does. Like he's gray. And maybe fifty and change."

"Umm." Carlie frowned and squeezed her eyes closed. "I'm not getting the attraction."

"Well, me neither. I'm not exactly attracted to him, but I liked him. Super cool guy. Nice. Funny."

The bell over the door dinged and drew Carlie's attention away from her computer screen.

"Sorry. We're closing in about five—"

Ben Sager shoved his hands in the pockets of his tight, worn jeans and met her eyes with a defiant tilt of his chin.

"Hey." She cleared her throat, aware that her heart was pounding so hard now that he could probably hear it. Hell, Erin could probably hear it. He nodded but said nothing.

"Was that hey for me? Because it sounded sort of swoon—ohmygod, Carlie! Is he there? Is B—"

Eyes still locked with Ben's, Carlie swiped her phone up and took it off speaker phone.

"Hey. Can I call you back?" She turned her head and spun her chair around to give Ben her back.

"Is he there?" Erin repeated.

"Are you going to see him again?" Carlie asked, desperate to make Ben think they were talking about anything but him.

"Maybe." Erin sighed. "Haven't decided."

"I'm a little bit weirded out by that."

"I'm not thinking about sleeping with him. He asked if I wanted to see a movie."

"You know where this is leading, E. He's a guy."

"Call me later," Erin instructed her.

"Yeah—"

The phone went dead in her hand. Carlie took a quick breath to calm her nerves—too bad it backfired and kick-started the butterflies in her belly. With surprisingly steady hands, she set her phone on her desk. Not wanting to feel at a disadvantage or awkward looking up at Ben, she stood and smoothed her hands over her thighs before turning to him.

"Erin?" he asked. His voice was gruff and edgy again, and for a second, Carlie was jealous that it was her friend's name on his lips and not hers. But the way he looked at her soothed the ruffled feathers. Ben's bedroom eyes devoured her—painstakingly slow, like a wolf sizing up his dinner.

Unable to find her voice, Carlie gave him a quick nod.

"Was she talking about me?"

Her heart might have sprouted wings; it took flight in her chest and climbed her throat as he approached her desk. The worn denim stretched tight around his thighs and cupped his groin, making her fingers quiver with excitement.

"What're you doing here?" she asked him, pleased that she didn't sound breathless or timid.

Ben shrugged; the open zipper of his coat moving with him, drawing Carlie's eyes from his legs and up to his chest. The navy thermal tee he wore looked soft and inviting.

"I thought I would see if you were free for dinner."

Carlie licked her lips and then bit her tongue, before she could ask him to repeat himself.

"Are you asking me out?"

Another careless shrug. "Dinner."

She nodded. "Yeah." She cleared her throat and looked around the deep, but narrow office space. Sandy was nowhere in sight. Carlie's nerves flared; heat stroked her belly and tingled through her thighs. Her core.

Were they really doing this?

"Let me get my things."

"Take your time."

# THIRTEEN

"Where are we going?"

Ben held the door open for her and nudged her when she stood next to him on the sidewalk.

"Zip up. It's cold out here."

"Are you always this bossy?"

"Damn straight."

They walked side by side, Ben leading Carlie to his truck. When they neared it, he nodded at the black 4x4. "This okay?"

Carlie's eyes widened when she looked back at him. *Jesus, was she scared to get in the truck with him? What happened to the sexy little flirt who had sent the text saying she wasn't all that into nice guys?*

Then again, he hadn't believed that the first time he read it, and reading it seventeen times since then hadn't changed his mind. Carlie Beringer was a sweet little thing who had no idea the fire she was playing with.

"What about my car?" She turned to him and tipped her head.

Her car? That's what she was worried about?

"I'll bring you back here to get it," he promised her.

"Okay."

Ben pressed his hand to her lower back and ushered her to the passenger side of the truck. He felt her eyes on him as he beeped the key fob and reached for the handle. Carlie moved toward the truck as he started to open the door. So close now they were almost touching, Ben took a moment to study her face. Her cheekbones were sharper than he remembered, the hollows below her cheeks alluring.

He took a moment to notice her parted lips, the tip of her tongue when it touched the center of her upper lip. Not trusting himself to stop if he kissed her now, Ben gave himself a mental shake and pulled the door open. Carlie stood frozen for a moment, watching him—her eyes roving over his face and his lips. Ben snapped his mouth shut on an impatient sigh; his dick stirring at Carlie's intense gaze. When he thought he couldn't stand it a second longer, she moved, slipping further by him and climbing into the truck.

"Where are we going?" she asked again when he was settled in the driver's seat.

"Do you like Chinese food?"

"Yes! But that's not an answer!" She tossed her little black purse on the floor by her feet and buckled her seatbelt, watching him with wide eyes all the while. A little pang of something foreign hit him in the chest—he loved the sparkle in her eyes and the easy smile she offered him. "Where are you taking me?"

"It's just a little hole in the wall place." He started the

truck, dropped it in gear, and slowly eased out of the parking space. "No atmosphere, but it's the best Chinese food in town."

When she didn't answer, he glanced at her and studied her as she gazed out the windshield. Something in the way she sat, chin high and eyes roving the street in front of them, made her seem excited and ready for something fun to happen any minute.

Ben looked away. He would only disappoint her.

"What're you thinking?" Her question broke the silence that had settled over them.

"I like your smile."

Where the hell had that come from? Because while he did like her smile, that sure as hell wasn't what he was thinking. More like how badly he wanted to undress her. Kiss her soft, innocent skin. Bury himself in her heat and make her scream his name. That once he made her come—and he would be happy to play between her legs all night long—he would have nothing left to offer her. A shithole apartment. Baggage in the form of an ex-wife and child support payments. Shared custody of a little girl. A drinking problem that had driven Heather away, so why in the hell would this woman want to stick around?

Still, now that he had said it, he wanted to see her reaction. He peeked at her and then looked back at the road. She didn't look offended, but she was definitely thinking something over.

"What?" he finally asked.

"I like your eyes."

Ben glanced at her again, ready to argue with her.

Ready to defend himself for saying he liked her smile—complimenting a woman in this day and age was sometimes the wrong thing to do.

"You what?" He tipped his head, remembered he was driving, and looked back at the street.

"I like your eyes."

"My eyes," he repeated almost silently. "You like my eyes?"

"I do."

"Hmm." He nodded. Heather was the only woman to ever tell him she liked his eyes. The women he'd been with since the divorce liked his body, specifically his dick. Ben wasn't sure what to think about Carlie's comment.

"What's your favorite entrée?"

"Kung pao chicken." Ben flipped the radio on. "You?"

"Sesame chicken and lo mein."

"What do you listen to?" He nodded toward the radio. "If you say podcasts, I'm dumping you out at the next corner."

Carlie snorted. "I do more audio books than podcasts," she told him. "But I like classic rock."

"Yeah?" He grinned. "Favorite band?"

"Pink Floyd."

"Really?" He tapped his fingers on the steering wheel and considered her answer. "What about Led Zeppelin?"

"Yeah." She nodded.

"You can change that."

"So, you must listen to country."

The current station was a country station, and he did listen to country music at times. Right now, it was tuned there because he had listened to local news earlier and never bothered to change it.

"Some."

He drove another few minutes without talking. Carlie fiddled with the radio and finally settled on a classic rock station playing a Marshall Tucker Band song.

"Why Pink Floyd?"

When he snuck a look at her this time, she was nibbling on her lower lip. She frowned, lost in thought, and shrugged. "My dad listened to them a lot when I was younger."

"Your dad again," he teased.

"A daddy is every little girl's first love."

The *l* word made him twitch a little bit in his seat, but he didn't comment. Her words made him think about Naomi.

"Mmm." He pursed his lips as he made a left off Main Street and pulled the truck into a tiny lot off Third. "Naomi loves her Papa."

"Is that what she calls you?"

He shook his head and threw his seatbelt off.

"Heather's dad."

He jumped out of the truck quickly, ready to put an end to that conversation. Carlie seemed willing to drop it when he opened her door and offered her a hand. She grabbed onto him, her skin on his sending fireworks through his blood. He eyed her closely as she reached back into the truck to grab her purse. She didn't seem to notice the way her touch affected him.

Didn't seem too affected by touching him, either.

And yet, she had at least mentioned him to her friend Erin.

"How's your back?" he asked as they walked around the truck to the sidewalk.

"Good days and bad," she answered. "Had physical therapy yesterday."

"Does that make it hurt?"

She nodded and shrugged as he pulled the door of the restaurant open for her. Ben watched her, fascinated by the way she took everything in, the constant searching, looking, noticing anything and everything. The way her lips were always a second away from a smile.

"Yeah, but I'm okay."

"Are you hungry?"

She looked up at him over her shoulder and hit him with a shy smile. Knees weak from the look, Ben cleared his throat and nodded for her to go ahead of him into the tiny dining room.

"I am," she answered, her face a mask of innocence now. "Hungry."

There was no sign to say so, but Ben had been there often enough to know they were to seat themselves. He reached for her, let his hand trail down her arm, and finally linked his fingers with hers. Carlie followed him without hesitation. The place was dead, but he knew it would fill up quickly with the dinner hour just starting.

"I've never heard of this place," Carlie announced once they were at a round two-top table tucked away in the far corner of the room. She shrugged out of her coat and hung it over the back of her chair.

CHAPTER

# FOURTEEN

"Crab Rangoon or egg rolls?" Ben asked when they were seated.

"Why choose?" Carlie tipped her head and narrowed her eyes at him. She did like both, but there was no way she was hungry enough to go all in with more than one appetizer and an entrée, too. She'd said it to get a reaction out of him, thrilled when Ben rewarded her with a hearty laugh.

He looked different when he laughed, Carlie decided. Always sexy, but the laughter shook the tension from his shoulders and eased the worry around his eyes. As much as she appreciated the dark and brooding look, the relaxed, content look was even more appealing.

"Alright." He nodded and looked around, presumably for their waitress. "The lady is hungry tonight."

Carlie felt her cheeks flush when his intense gaze landed back on her face. He was teasing her; she knew that. She was a little bit hungry for dinner, but the more time she spent in his company, the hungrier she grew for a taste of him.

"I'm not," she argued with a grin. "I mean, I am. But no, don't order both. I just wanted to see what you would say."

"You ask me for something, Carlie Beringer, and I'm going to deliver."

Her mouth suddenly dry, she fought her desire to look away. Ben devoured her with those bedroom eyes, making Carlie wiggle in her chair. Thankfully, their waitress chose that moment to approach them and ask for their order. The older woman was friendly without being too talkative, and yet, watching Ben talk to her told her he was here enough that she recognized him.

Once they had ordered and they were alone again, Carlie steeled herself for the answer and dived in with the question.

"Did you come here a lot with your ex-wife?"

The tiny wince on his face made her heart hurt, but she wasn't sure why. After all, she wasn't sure what he was feeling. Regret that he was divorced? Loneliness for his ex? Or maybe just guilt for bringing Carlie somewhere his ex might have liked.

"Heather and I were here now and then," he answered, "but I've been in here at least once a week since the divorce."

"How long has it been?" Carlie's voice was gruff with that hurt in her heart, but she still didn't understand it.

"A year," he said with a sigh.

"And how old is your little girl?"

His smile lit up his face, his eyes flickering with happiness.

"Three."

"Do you see her often?"

Carlie was asking about his daughter, and yet as the words tumbled out, she realized she wanted, needed, to know if he saw his ex-wife often.

"We share custody," he answered. "It's a tough schedule with my job."

"I'm sure it is," she agreed. The waitress appeared with their drinks—Japanese beers. Carlie had followed Ben's lead when they ordered. She took a swig from the longneck bottle now and decided it wasn't bad.

"We parted as friends. So, it's not like we have big ugly fights about Naomi."

"Then why are you divorced?" she asked boldly.

"The job," he offered with a shrug. "Happens a lot."

"Maybe." She nodded.

"I drink a lot." He threw the words down, almost like a gauntlet, at her feet.

Carlie stared at him silently for several moments. She hadn't seen evidence of that; Ben didn't strike her as a man who drank enough to drive his wife away. Then again, she hadn't been around him much at all. Her belly flip-flopped with nerves. She liked him. Ben was warning her off again, but she wasn't ready to cut and run just yet.

"She left you?"

Another wince, and then he sat back in his chair and folded his arms over his chest. Was he pushing her away? Putting that space between them for a reason?

"I left her," he said quietly. "She was miserable. She deserves better."

Carlie nodded. Ben Sager was broken. She had no idea what had done it, what had left him dark and broody. But she ached to slip around the table and put her arms around him. Broken people needed, deserved, love and understanding just the same as everyone else.

Sensing that it was time to change the subject, that any further talk about Heather and his marriage right now might make him clam up, might change the way tonight ended, Carlie looked around the small room again.

"Why Led Zeppelin?"

"What?" Ben asked with a frown.

"You asked if I liked Led Zeppelin, so I assume you do." She shrugged. "Why?"

"Good music."

Ben moved again, leaning closer and resting his folded arms on the table.

"What about your mom?" he asked her.

"She doesn't bench, but she's run a couple of marathons."

Ben's laugh filled her with something light, almost effervescent. Bubbly and hoping for more, she gave him a goofy smile and then scrunched her nose up to continue, "She likes easy-listening music."

"And you don't?"

"Depends on my mood, I guess, but not usually."

"And you?"

"I haven't tried to bench press anything since high school PE classes. Back then, I could barely lift the bar."

Ben held his bottle at his lips and studied her face. Clearly amused at her admission, he took a drink and put the bottle down.

"And now?"

"I can do pull-ups. Like ten of them."

Well, she used to be able to do ten good pull-ups. But that was before the accident. She had no idea what her body could or would do now. She was still doing physical therapy for her injuries; no telling when she would be able to go back to working out.

"Where'd you go?"

"Hmm?" She jerked her gaze back to meet his eyes.

"Just now. You got all dark and gloomy."

Carlie worked her lower lip with her teeth. "I haven't worked out since before the accident. No idea what I can do these days."

Ben started to say something, but the waitress appeared with their orders. Carlie pushed the discomfort down her throat and studied her dinner. The lo mein looked delicious. She worried now that she wouldn't be able to eat much. Not with the accident at the table with them.

"You've come a long way," he told her a few moments later.

"What?"

"You had some serious injuries," he reminded her. "I know your family was worried you wouldn't walk—"

"You met my family?"

"Not really." He reached for his beer but changed his mind and picked up his water for a drink. "There was a couple there that I assumed were your parents the first time I was there. I just told them..."

"That you were the one to cut me out of the car."

Ben stared at her unapologetically.

"Is that okay?"

"Is what okay?"

"That I was there?"

Carlie huffed out a sigh. She felt the weight of his stare as she nibbled on her chicken and then a bite of the lo mein.

"It makes me feel kind of...weird."

"Weird like what?" he insisted. "Tell me."

Carlie could almost see the tension tightening up his shoulders and his neck. He straightened now in his chair and watched her closely.

"I dunno." She swallowed hard and looked around the table, as if she would find the words to explain how she felt written there. "Vulnerable. I mean, obviously you saw me at my worst. Half-dead—"

She stopped talking when Ben reached over the table and covered her hand with his.

"I don't wanna be weak," she said softly. "I don't want anyone to see me that way."

"I see a beautiful, resilient woman when I look at you."

"And I think you might need glasses." She jumped at the opportunity to make light of what he had said to her.

"Eat your dinner." He lifted his hand from hers and waved it at her plate. "Good nutrition and plenty of rest. Just what the doctor ordered."

CHAPTER

# FIFTEEN

B en listened quietly as Carlie shared a travel story involving her friend Erin, bad shrimp, and a long night for Carlie and Erin in a beach front hotel room. He and Heather used to talk like this, but he realized as he listened to the ups and downs in Carlie's tones, the soft laughter as she spoke, he had tuned Heather out somewhere along the line. No, he didn't think turning back time and listening to his ex-wife share memories and laughter with him would magically fix things. But as he helped Carlie back into his truck, it dawned on him that he missed these kinds of nights.

Fun conversation. Some teasing. Flirting. Laughing.

He liked more about Carlie than he planned to, and he wasn't sure what to think about that.

On the drive back to the travel agency to retrieve her car, Ben changed the station to something country, mostly to see what Carlie would do. He figured she would growl at him at the least and possibly even change it back. Instead, he was surprised to hear her singing along with an older Martina McBride song.

Maybe she wouldn't go far on *The Voice*, but he loved hearing her sing just the same.

"Thanks for dinner," she told him when he pulled into the lot where he had picked her up.

"You're welcome." He nodded. "Which car is yours?"

Ben swung his truck into a space next to the compact car she pointed at, shoving aside the image of a broken and bleeding Carlie, trapped in a smashed-up SUV. She opened her door as soon as he killed the engine, leaving Ben to wonder if she was in a hurry to get away from him. Still, he took his time unbuckling his own seatbelt and opening his door. By the time he rounded the truck and stood at her door, she had turned her legs sideways to hop down. Once again, Ben offered her his hand, ridiculously pleased when she took it.

He waited patiently when she turned to grab her purse and swung the door closed once she had stepped aside.

"I see people now and then," he told her as they approached her car. Tucking his hands in his pockets again, he studied the ground as they walked. The weight of her stare kindled a little fire of nerves in his gut. "From accidents."

They stopped walking at her driver's door, but neither of them moved except to turn to each other. Carlie stared at him expectantly.

"Some are just faces that seem familiar," he continued. "Some of them—I know their names. Maybe I know they have a kid at home. Or a cat." He shrugged uncomfortably.

"And?"

"You asked me the other day if I texted other—"

"Accident victims," she supplied the words for him, a brow arched sharply, her voice a little bit prickly.

"Of course I don't," he went on, ignoring her attempt to put him off. He knew the skill well; he used a belligerent attitude often enough to shove people away when he was in a foul mood.

"Do you visit them in the hospital?" She tipped her head expectantly and watched him closely.

"Yeah." He nodded. "But not like...not like I did with you."

"What does that mean?"

"I can't get you outta my head." He cupped her chin in his hand and lowered his eyes to her lips. "And I'm not sure how to feel about that."

"Are you going to kiss me?" she whispered.

*Leave it to Carlie to come right out and ask him.* He grinned and dropped his head back to look at the sky.

"Well, you did say if I asked for something, you would deliver," she reminded him.

"I did say that, didn't I?" He met her eyes again and nodded.

"And maybe if you kissed me, you would have a better idea how to feel about not getting me out of your—"

Ben cut her off with a barely-there press of his lips to hers. Just a feather light touch of his skin on hers, but he lingered there, breathing in her sweet, flowery scent.

"Is there—"

"Shhh." He stroked his fingers over her cheek and around to cup the back of her head. Drawing her closer, he kissed the corner of her mouth and left a trail of soft, chaste kisses over her cheek.

"I won't break," she whispered.

She probably wouldn't. And if he were honest with her, he would have to admit that earlier he thought he wanted to strip her down and bang her on the hood of her car. Hell, when he first picked her up earlier, he would have liked to bend her over her desk and take her hard and fast. Now that he was close to her, now that they had shared dinner together—now that he knew she liked lo mein rather than fried rice and she knew the words to "Independence Day" and she sensed when to push him to talk and when to back pedal—now he wanted to cherish her.

"Good to know." He kissed her forehead and drew back enough to look her in the eyes. She held his gaze, silently waiting for him to say more. Maybe to kiss her again. Ben played with her hair for a moment, finally leaning close again and claiming her lips in another soft, sweet kiss.

Surprise and longing flooded him when he felt her hand inching up his arm. Her touch was light through his coat, but he felt her fingers curl around his upper arm and squeeze gently. Her breath was hot on his lips. He peeked at her to see that her eyes were closed, her long lashes dark on her porcelain face.

She trusted him.

She'd gone with him for dinner when he'd shown up

unannounced earlier. She'd climbed into his truck and assumed he would take her somewhere and feed her, treat her with kindness. She'd shared bits of her life with him, and she'd looped her fingers through his, and she'd sung along to a song on the radio while riding in his truck.

And now, standing toe to toe with him, she closed her eyes waiting for him to kiss her again.

Her hair was silk in his hand. Ben imagined the dark blond waves spread over her pillow as he kissed his way down her throat. Hanging around her face as she rode atop him, both aching for sweet release.

"Ben?"

Her whisper drew him back to the here and now. Before she could move, Ben lifted his other hand to her face and touched her lips with his fingertips. He still wasn't sure how he felt about the way he wanted her. The way that raging desire to strip her down and fuck her had simmered into a painful need to worship her.

With his heartbeat thrumming in his ears, his throat, Ben opened his mouth and scraped his teeth over her lip. Her soft sweet gasp of pleasure went straight to his heart.

"Please."

The gruff plea spurred him into action. His lips on hers again, he stroked her teeth with his tongue and dived into the heat of her mouth when she invited him. Still gentle, still deliciously slow and curious, their tongues slid together over and over. Ben was suddenly aware of Carlie's fingers on his neck, the heat from her skin searing him, pain and pleasure raging in his belly, his blood.

He could drag her back to his truck and make use of that backseat. He could drive her to his apartment or her place. She wanted him the same way he wanted her. But he didn't want to rush through a crazy, stupid fling with Carlie Beringer. He wanted this thrill, the high he felt with her, to last a little while.

She licked her lips when he drew away from her, her moony eyes on his face. Ben waited a moment to speak, a little out of breath from the kiss and how it revved his body up for more. Pleased to see Carlie seemed to be a little breathless, too, he pressed his thumb to her lips.

"Goodnight, Carlie."

Frozen, she stared at him for a moment and finally gave him a quick nod.

"Goodnight, Ben."

Still, she didn't move.

"Get in." He tipped his head toward her vehicle, aware of the way her eyes tracked the smirk on his face. "I'll follow you home."

"You don't have to do that."

"I know I don't," he said quietly. "But I'm going to."

Finally, she huffed out a sigh, nodded, and stepped around him to unlock her door.

"Carlie?" He leaned in when she looked at him over her shoulder. He stole this kiss, moving close and flicking her lips, her tongue, with his, and then stepped back and jammed his hands in his pockets to watch her get in.

"So." She rolled her window down as she started the car. Ben's belly stretched with dread when she stared silently at the steering wheel, a frown marring her fore-head. "What is this? What're we doing?"

Hell if he knew.

Knowing an answer like that would hurt her, he leaned his elbows on the open window frame and rested his forehead on the car door.

"I don't know."

She nodded. Swallowed hard and dropped her head back to rest on the driver's seat. Ben watched the emotions wash over her face and wished he had the right to ask her what she was thinking.

"Am I gonna see you again?" She blinked and looked at him without moving.

Instead of answering her, he leaned in the window and kissed her again. A sweet, gentle kiss that he hoped would linger for a long time. Maybe forever.

"You should run from me," he whispered as he backed away from the window and straightened. Carlie sat up and watched him for a moment, putting the window up when she realized he wasn't going to say more.

He didn't know if she would throw the car into gear and get out of the lot before he got back in his truck. But he didn't hurry. In fact, he walked backwards, unwilling to look away from her. She watched, lips pressed together, until he pulled his door open and climbed inside the truck again.

She made a left out of the parking lot and drove just over the speed limit until she hit Fourteenth Street and made a right. Ben eyed the houses curiously as she slowed and pulled her car to the curb in front of a little bungalow. He made a mental note of her address, though it made him feel a little creepy to do so. What would she do if he showed up *here* unannounced?

He put the truck in park, there in the middle of Birch Street, and waited while she climbed out, grabbed her purse, and swung her door closed. She beeped the lock on her car, turned to look at him, to stare him down, and then turned to the sidewalk. He wanted to stay. To sit here all night and watch her house.

No, he didn't. He wanted to be invited in.

Into her home.

Her bed.

He wanted to be inside *her*. But Carlie Beringer was different from the other women he'd been with since he and Heather divorced. She might read more into a night of sex.

And Ben wasn't the kind of guy for more.

CHAPTER

# SIXTEEN

Naomi poured him another cup of tea and handed it back to him with her trademark grin. The kid was happy; she was always smiling and laughing about something. Ben's heart ached with joy to watch his little girl play make-believe as she always did.

"Do you like your tea, Daddy?" she asked from her spot on the floor. Ben took in her fuzzy socks, leggings, and princess sweatshirt. She knelt on the opposite side of the coffee table from him, her folded arms resting on the table itself. Curls that had slipped loose of the ponytail framed her face. Her chipmunk cheeks were pink with health.

"I love my tea, Naomi," he promised her.

"Do you want anything else?" Heather asked him.

The dinner date with Carlie two nights ago had left him unsettled. Disgusted with himself for the X-rated thoughts he had about her. She was so young. Someone else's daughter. He'd stood in Carlie's hospital room with her parents and looked them in the eyes and said he was so thankful she had survived the accident. Now he wanted to get in her pants.

Except, he wanted more, and he didn't even know what that more was. Or why he wanted it, and mostly, he didn't deserve it. He liked Carlie. Lunch with her at Beanstalks had been kind of fun. He had been entertained by her scoop on why women liked fancy cups and water bottles. No, they hadn't exactly bonded over that, but it had made him curious about her. Listening to her talk about her friend Erin and their trips, listening to her sing Martina McBride—it made him curious.

He wanted to know more about her. He wanted more than hot, dirty sex and a kiss goodbye. But he didn't know *what* he wanted, and that wasn't fair to anyone.

"No. Thanks." He tipped his head back and smiled at Heather when she climbed from the couch. Because he felt off, uncertain about Carlie, he had avoided seeing her for a couple of days. And then wrestled with feeling guilty about that. To Carlie's credit, she hadn't called him or nagged him about seeing him.

They had texted quite a bit since the dinner date. Carlie had started those texts, but she didn't even mention the kiss. Instead, she sent him a GIF of someone banging his head against a wall. Even with no context, it had made Ben laugh. He texted back to ask if she was having a bad day, laughing more when she told him she was trying to plan a trip for an older couple who was so concerned about pinching pennies they balked at every activity or event Carlie suggested.

"Bath time, baby girl." Heather gave Naomi's ponytail a gentle tug.

"Will Daddy stay?" Naomi asked Heather, but her eyes were locked on his.

"I will." He nodded, cringing when his little girl jumped up with excitement and nearly knocked Heather off her feet. Naomi threw herself into his lap and wound her arms around his neck. "That okay?" He glanced at Heather hopefully.

"Sure. You wanna get her in the tub? I'll pick the toys up and get her jammies."

"I'm wearing my WeeLo and Stitch jammies now," Naomi informed him.

"What happened to the *Frozen* jammies?" He climbed to his feet effortlessly, Naomi still glued to him like a postage stamp.

"Mommy said she had to worsh them."

"Wash them," Heather corrected her.

"Yep." Naomi looked back at Ben. She puckered up and smacked a kiss on his cheek. "Daddy, you gots whiskers."

He cut a look to Heather, who smiled and arched her brows, and then turned away. Heather used to tell him she liked his scruffy face.

Ben couldn't bring himself to flirt back. Not tonight. In fact, he hadn't had that kind of interaction with Heather in several weeks now. Not even on her birthday. He'd taken her and Naomi out for pizza, and they had cake. But after they put Naomi to bed, and Heather looped her arms around his neck, Ben was ready to go home.

There wasn't a lot of room in the tub for Naomi, not with all the toys she kept there. He remembered the days of stepping around rubber duckies and bathtub chalk when he showered here. When he lived here. Tonight, Naomi played with cups, pouring water from one to the other and back. Ben took in her chubby little thighs and toes and the pink paint on her toenails and felt a stab of love so fierce, it took his breath away. His little girl was perfect.

And he owed so much of that, so much of who Naomi was and how healthy and happy she was, to his ex-wife. Ben sat on the closed toilet lid while Heather bathed her. He and Naomi sang a few verses of "Down by the Bay," and Heather howled at their performance like a dog.

"Daddy, I'm goin' to be a song singer," Naomi told him as Heather toweled her off. Ben narrowed his eyes at her and tapped his finger on his chin.

"Well, I think you'd be a fine song singer when you get bigger," he decided. "But I thought you wanted to be Wonder Woman."

"I'm going to be a song singing Wonder Woman." Naomi nodded.

"Yesterday, you told me you were going to be a puppy doctor," Heather reminded her. Ben watched Heather slather lotion over Naomi's fair skin and then help her step into her little pink underpants—this pair had strawberries on the seat—and finally, her *Lilo and Stitch* nightgown.

"Will you read a story, Daddy?" she asked when Heather picked her up and sat her on the edge of the sink.

"What should we read?" He twisted around and

rested his folded arms on the sink by Naomi's leg and then propped his chin on his arms.

"The one about the grubs," Naomi whispered. Ben snorted and moved only his eyes to look at Heather. She was grinning as she put a bit of toothpaste on Naomi's brush.

"No Billy Goats Gruff," Heather argued.

"I wike it, though," Naomi whined.

"It scares you, Naomi."

"Not when my daddy reads it to me." Naomi reached over to pat Ben's head. A low, lazy laugh rumbled up from his belly.

"Brush your teeth, and I'll read Goldilocks."

Naomi opened her mouth and looked at Heather expectantly. Before Heather could start brushing her teeth, she peeked at Ben and whispered, "And the grubs."

"So." Heather cleared her throat and tipped her head at him. Ben felt like a jackass as he pulled his coat on. She had fixed dinner for him; they'd had a good night—the tea party with Naomi the best part. But he was ready to get home. He wanted to talk to Carlie.

On Heather's birthday, he had brushed a quick, chaste kiss over her cheek. Since then, he'd been careful not to get too close to her. Not because he didn't trust himself; but because he couldn't get Carlie out of his head. That wasn't a lie he told Carlie, no come-on line. No, Ben had kept his distance from Heather because she wanted him to stick around again. He knew her well enough to know what she wanted. He couldn't have sex with her when he was thinking about Carlie. He might be a dick, but he wasn't *that* guy. That was no way to treat either of them.

"Thanks for dinner," he said again.

"What's going on?"

"Ready to get home," he told her, knowing it wasn't enough. That he would have to come clean with her soon enough. "Thanks for letting me stick around and read to Naomi."

Heather laughed softly. "She'll be in my bed tonight."

"Seriously?"

"The grubs scare her," she said with a shrug, the tired smile still on her face. Still attractive to Ben. But she wasn't Carlie, either. As much as he liked hanging out with Heather, Ben had found himself wondering tonight what had happened with Carlie's penny-pinching clients.

"I think it's adorable that she calls the trolls grubs." Ben stuck his hands in his pockets. The door was at his back. His keys were in his pocket. He could text Carlie from his truck. Call her when he got home.

"Sure, it's adorable, to you." Heather nodded. "You're not the one telling her at two a.m. that grubs and trolls, neither one, exist, and that billy goats don't talk."

"I don't think I like the idea of scary grubs," Ben admitted with a shiver.

"Is there someone else?"

Out of the blue like that, Heather's question caught him totally off guard.

"What?"

"You've been blowing me off since my birthday."

"You deserve—"

"Cut the shit, Ben." Heather rolled her eyes. "For God's sake, it's not like it's even cheating. But something's changed. You could just tell me."

Ben held her gaze for a moment and finally looked away.

"Who is she?"

"I don't know."

Frustrated, he pushed away from the door, stepped around Heather, and ran a hand over the top of his head.

"You don't know? What? You've got a thing for a stranger you saw on the bus?"

Heather's sarcasm might have been deserved, but it stung just the same.

"Don't be like that, Heather," he said softly. Back to her, he huffed out a harsh sigh and smoothed his hand over the back of his head to cup his neck.

"Oh." Still heavy with sarcasm. "So. What? Who is she?"

"Her name's Carlie."

"Car—" Heather stopped and cleared her throat. "Carlie."

Ben looked up and dropped his hand when she pushed away from the door and dropped in a heap on the couch.

"She's..." He clenched his teeth and breathed deeply through his nose. He shouldn't be doing this. He shouldn't be telling Heather about some woman who had turned his head. Maybe if the divorce was five years in the past and Heather was happily remarried. Maybe then. As it was, it felt wrong to confide in his ex-wife.

But he needed to talk about this. To someone.

"What?"

At the throb in her tone, Ben looked closely and realized she was crying.

"Heather."

"No, no." She shook her head. "I'm okay."

"I don't even know...what we're doing. I don't know."

"Where'd you meet her?"

Ben hesitated, frozen there on the opposite side of the coffee table from where he'd been only an hour ago having pretend tea with Naomi.

"She was in a car accident."

The silence in the room was painfully thick, so heavy Ben couldn't get a deep breath. When he looked at Heather, she leaned forward, as if she was straining to hear him.

"A couple of months ago. Stayed in the hospital for a while with serious injuries."

"Jesus Christ." Heather flinched. "You saved her? You pulled her out of the wreck?"

Ben answered with a begrudging nod.

"Are you sleeping with her?"

"No."

"Ben."

"No. We've just..." Ben turned away from Heather's heavy stare, a little embarrassed to feel so undone. For his ex-wife to *see* him so undone for someone else. "I visited her. After the accident."

"And now it's happily-ever-after?" She arched an eyebrow, clearly skeptical.

"No. I just needed to see her. She looked young, so broken. I went to make sure her boyfriend was there. That someone was there to comfort her."

"Boyfriend?"

Ben huffed again. "Long story."

"Well, at least you're in good shape."

"What does that mean?" Ben turned to face her and propped a shoulder on the wall at his back.

"If her boyfriend decides to come after you and beat your ass—"

"She doesn't have a boyfriend."

Heather eyed him silently. The dried tears on her face made her look more miserable somehow.

"Ben." She closed her eyes.

"I'm sorry, Heather."

"Baby, I'm worried about you." Heather stood and moved around the coffee table to stand closer to him. She stopped a few feet away though, careful not to touch him. Careful to keep her distance.

"Why are you worried about me?"

"You're a big, badass firefighter, Ben." She tipped her head, her eyes pleading with him to listen. "You're sexy as hell. You pulled her out of a wreck and got her to a hospital."

Ben hung his head and squeezed his eyes closed.

Yes, the thought had crossed his mind. And he'd chased it away, because he didn't know what *he felt for Carlie. What he wanted.*

Only that he did.

Want.

To be around her. With her.

Special to her.

If he couldn't understand his feelings, he couldn't be suspicious of Carlie's.

"Jesus, Ben. I don't know what you're thinking, but I know you're feeling something for this woman."

Lips pressed firmly together, Ben lifted his head and met Heather's eyes.

"What if it's just hero worship?" she whispered.

"What if it's just me? Wanting to be someone's hero again?"

# CHAPTER
# SEVENTEEN

Carlie didn't know what to make of the impromptu dinner date with Ben. Or the goodnight kiss. She'd had fun. Spending the evening with him, talking to him —as impromptu dates with hot guys went, it was at the top of her list. She'd dated some good-looking guys, and she'd dated popular guys now and then in school. But there was something about Ben that was different. More intense. More intriguing.

*More.*

She wanted more. More time with him. Another dinner. Lunch. A movie. She wanted to talk to him, *converse with him.* Not about life-shattering moments, but everyday stuff. He'd watched her with intense eyes that night they went out, listening attentively to everything she said. His lips had perked up often in amusement. He'd made comments here and there, but mostly he'd been quiet. As sexy as the dark, brooding thing was, Carlie wanted to hack away at the wall around him and learn what made him tick.

And while she was at it, she would like more kissing.

He hadn't exactly left her hanging after that night. They spoke through texts—sometimes actual text messages to share something funny or interesting about their days. Ben had texted her about seeing a little boy and a dog playing in what amounted to be a very light snow a few nights ago. She'd told him about Erin's weird coffee dates with the George-Clooney-look-alike guy. But they sent each other memes, too. Silly things to make each other laugh.

What she knew for sure was that when she sent any texts to Ben, it was because she was thinking about him. So, she decided to assume when he texted her, it was because he was thinking about her. And for now, that would be enough. He would call or show up again when he had time and he was ready to see her.

Still, her dreams were a wild mix of his bedroom eyes and his sexy, gruff voice. Sometimes, she was looking at him through the window of her SUV, when his steady gaze had kept her calm, given her comfort when she was scared. And sometimes, those eyes were closed, and his lips were open and on hers.

Only to break away and tell her again that she should run.

"So. Let me get this straight." Carlie aimed a frown at Erin and sipped from her smoothie. "You're going to dinner with him now."

Erin crunched a cracker as she nodded. "Yep."

"Okay. So, Leon." Carlie glanced at Erin's phone. "Leon is in his fifties, and you're going to have dinner with him."

"Stop!" Erin reached over the table and swatted at Carlie. She was happy. Maybe Carlie didn't get it, but she had to admit it had been a long time since she'd seen her friend happy like this. "He's not in his fifties. He just *turned* fifty."

Carlie pointed at Erin, ready to remind her friend that she wasn't even thirty, but Erin shook her head and continued.

"And it's just dinner."

"Erin." Carlie rolled her eyes. "Jeez, if you wanna sleep with him, sleep with him. It just seems crazy."

"Dinner," Erin repeated.

"Hey."

Shivers racked her body when she heard the baritone voice behind her. Ben. Ben, who wasn't a regular at Beanstalks, which meant he was here looking for her again.

"Hey." She looked up over her shoulder to meet his intense blue eyes. Heart pounding in her throat, she told herself to move, to say something. Thoughts of his lips on hers kept her frozen in place.

"Carlie?"

*Erin. Erin was here.*

Carlie gave herself a mental shake and peeked at her friend. What if Ben standing here beside her was her imagination, and when she looked back, he was gone?

"Ben," she said with a smile, "this is my friend Erin. Erin, this is Ben Sager."

"So, you're Ben."

When Carlie heard the little throb in Erin's voice, she tore her gaze away from Ben and focused on Erin. Good grief—she didn't need Erin rambling to this guy about the way Carlie was lusting after him.

"And you're Erin." Ben offered his hand and pumped Erin's when she took it. "It's nice to meet you."

"Thank you," Erin said quietly. Carlie almost kicked her under the table. "You're the guy who pulled her from the wreck, right?"

Ben nodded and shrugged the comment off. He tucked his hands in his pockets and shifted uneasily on his feet. Was he embarrassed about being called out for that? For doing his job? Or embarrassed to be talking to Carlie after the accident? The rescue?

"Carlie's been my person since we were kids," Erin explained. She cleared her throat. "Not ready to be done with her yet."

Ben's slow grin was like a drug, pounding through her body, warming her from the inside. Ratcheting up her heartbeat. Making her cheeks flush and her fingers tremble the slightest bit.

"I did the easy part," Ben told them, and before Carlie could react to that, he added, "Carlie had to do the fighting. The recovery."

"She's a fighter," Erin agreed.

"Sitting right here," she reminded them.

Erin tossed her fork down on her mostly eaten salad bowl.

"I should get going."

"Don't leave on my account." Ben frowned and looked around. Carlie felt her heart sink a bit. What if he wasn't here looking for her? What if he was here for lunch? Or to buy his ex-wife something else?

"Duty calls," Erin assured him as she stood and gathered her things. "Call you later."

"Oh, you better." Carlie nodded and watched her best friend all but run away from the table to leave her alone with Ben.

"I didn't mean to run her off." Ben looked from the door where Erin was stepping outside and back to Carlie.

"It's okay."

"Can I sit?"

"Yes."

"So, who does she want to sleep with?"

Carlie stared at Ben's hand, his fingers wrapped around the chair. He'd had his hands on her that night he kissed her. On her face. In her hair. The memory went straight to her core, making her squirm in her seat. What would those hands feel like on her skin? Her belly? Her breasts?

When he dropped into the chair and met her eyes, she looked away, certain he would read her mind.

"What?"

"I heard you tell her to sleep with him if she wanted to."

Interesting. Rather than discuss their kiss, Ben's warning, they were going to talk about Erin's weird thing with her not-boyfriend.

"She's been seeing some guy for coffee," Carlie answered with a frown. "And now he's asked her to dinner."

"And she wants to sleep with him?"

"She says she doesn't. But she's definitely going to dinner."

"Why doesn't she want to sleep with him?"

Carlie shrugged dramatically. "I don't know. Haven't met him. He's supposedly a George-Clooney-look-alike."

"George Clooney?" Ben quirked an eyebrow at her. "Is he your type?"

Carlie laughed softly. "I don't know if I have a type."

"But you're into Clooney?"

"Not necessarily." She shrugged. "He's good-looking, but I'm pretty sure the odds of me bumping into him aren't great."

That grin again. Their eyes locked; Carlie was suddenly breathless.

"You didn't run."

"I don't want to," she said simply.

Ben leaned his elbows on the table and rubbed his eyes. Carlie noticed a cut on his forearm, where his sleeve rode up. It didn't look life-threatening, but she had to remind herself grabbing his hand and tugging it close to kiss the cut here wasn't an option.

"I'm gone a lot. At the station house," he told her. She simply nodded. "I'm arrogant, I have a hero complex, and I don't like to lose."

"Okay."

Maybe now wasn't the best time for her to tell him she disagreed. He might not like to lose. He might be a perfectionist. But what he called arrogance translated to confidence for Carlie. And if he did have a bit of a swagger, Carlie was in awe of his body and the way it moved, so she took no issue with it.

"Every day I go to work, there's a possibility I won't come home."

She nodded. "That could be anyone, Ben."

"But the odds are a lot higher for me."

"I'm a dreamer. I've been told I'm obnoxious. I laugh a lot. I don't go to bed without thinking something good about my day."

Ben whooshed out an anguished sigh.

"I don't want to hurt you, Carlie."

"Then don't."

"If you don't want me to hurt you, I might as well walk away now."

"I'm a big girl, Ben," she reminded him. "And I'm not gonna break."

They sat in silence for a moment, Carlie's smoothie pushed aside.

"Dinner?"

He reached across the table and wrapped his fingers around hers, eyes pinning her in place.

"Come to my house," she told him.

She wasn't a gourmet chef, but she was functional in the kitchen. Some things she did rather well in the kitchen. And she didn't want another dinner date ending like the last one did.

"Are you sure?" His voice was gruff with longing.

"Come at six."

# CHAPTER
# EIGHTEEN

She had a neat little house. He hadn't paid a lot of attention the night he followed her home after dinner. Just a quick glance at the little bungalow. Tonight, he sat in his truck for a few seconds, eyes roaming the front of the house, admiring the porch just big enough for a chair and maybe a plant when the weather was right.

With a sigh, Ben glanced at the time on his phone. Minutes after six. He could have been here at six on the dot. He could have been here early. But he'd stewed over what he was doing. Carlie Beringer felt like a kid to him, and his interest in her bugged him. And yet, she held her own in conversation—hell, who was he kidding? She *led* their conversations, even when he tried to scare her off. She kissed like a grown woman who knew what she wanted from a man. And she had invited him here for dinner.

Ben had almost been tempted to talk to Heather about it. Did Carlie's invitation, her offer to do dinner at her place, mean she wanted to sleep with him? Was that going to happen tonight? *Jesus, Ben, you're being an idiot. Yes, she wants sex, and yes, the invitation to her home meant she wanted it to happen tonight.*

She wasn't a kid. She wasn't fragile. It was his problem that he had seen her vulnerable and needy. Not hers. Just to remind himself Carlie wasn't a kid, he thought about that goodnight kiss a few nights ago. Sweet, but sexy.

He wasn't sure he could be sweet with her. Hell, it had been way too long since he'd been sweet with Heather. Too much life had happened, and Ben wasn't some starry-eyed kid, thrilled to be in love anymore.

*Move.*

Before he could change his mind, he shoved his door open and slid out of the truck. Worn brown boots firmly on the ground, his knees felt a little weak.

What if it were Naomi? And some older guy was hitting on her?

"She's not a kid," he muttered to himself as he strode up the sidewalk to her porch. He hesitated on the first step when he heard music. Sounded like Bon Jovi. Had she been playing something soft and sexy, he might have turned around and left her alone. The eighties song currently playing reminded him Carlie was different. She marched to the beat of her own drum; she'd told him so right after he told her how bad he was.

Choosing to ignore the doorbell, he rapped his fist on the storm door and tipped his head down while he waited for her to answer. Already primed and ready to explode, his heart galloped when she pulled the door open, and he looked up to meet her eyes.

Dressed in faded skinny jeans and an oversized white button-up blouse, Carlie should have looked ordinary. Ben thought she looked good enough to eat. She'd pulled her hair up in a messy twist. A few curls had fallen loose to frame her face. Her eyelashes were so thick and long, he assumed she wore mascara. But that was it. No heavy eyeliner or shadow. She looked fifteen but a little bit immortal, too, like she knew things—things Ben would never dream of.

*Confidence.*

She faced him boldly and offered him a smile when she nodded for him to come in.

The tilt of her head and the sparkle in her eyes made him crazy for everything about her. Not just her slender hips and the slope of her neck.

"Hey."

When she leaned around him to close the door, Ben caught a breath of a sweet, floral scent. He bit off a curse when his dick jolted at her nearness.

"Hi."

He could smell something else, too. Dinner. Something a little garlicky. Heavenly.

He wanted her more.

A big dog—looked like an Aussie-German Shepherd mix—trotted forward to greet him.

"Hey." He held his hand out for the dog to sniff and then scratched its ears. "What's your name?"

"Nash."

Carlie's hand on his arm startled him. He nearly

jumped out of his skin. *Now? Were they going to just get right into it?* And why did that idea make him jumpy like a schoolgirl in a frat house?

"Let me take your coat," she told him when he looked at her. He wondered if he had a deer-in-the-headlights look as he shrugged it off. When she twisted to hook it on a coat tree by the wall, Ben caught a peek at the curve of her breast, visible over the top button of her blouse.

"I wasn't sure you would come."

Coat on the hook, she turned back and zapped him with her steady gaze.

"I wasn't sure I would either."

"Why wouldn't you?" She folded her arms over her chest and tipped her head to study him.

"I'm not sure this is a good idea."

"But why?"

"I'm too old for you."

"I'm old enough to make my own decisions."

"Carlie." He ground her name out through a clenched jaw.

"Twenty-five." She stepped closer to him. "Remember?"

He grinned despite himself.

"I'm old enough to live on my own," she whispered. Ben grunted when she touched his arm again. He closed his eyes as her fingers walked up his biceps and stopped on his shoulder. "Old enough to fix dinner. For me. And for you."

"It smells good," he admitted as he opened his eyes again.

"Old enough to do this."

Ben held himself rigid when she stepped closer and pressed her middle to his.

"You kissed me first," she reminded him.

"I know."

"Do you regret it?" She smoothed her fingers up the back of his neck and licked her lips.

"I think about it all the damned time," he answered, his voice low and hard.

"But do you regret it?"

"No."

"Then why don't you kiss me again?" She suggested, her lips twisting with a hint of a smile.

Like a dog, provoked to attack, Ben struck fast and smooth. One second his gaze was locked with hers and his hands were at his sides and the next, his fingers dug into her hips to yank her closer, and his mouth was on her neck. Rather than fight him, or even gasp in surprise, Carlie slid her arms over his shoulders and tipped her head back offering him more soft pale skin.

Ben stilled when the dog growled a low, guttural warning.

"See? Your dog knows I'm not good for you."

He nipped at her neck before pulling away to look first at the dog and then at her.

"He's just jealous," Carlie promised Ben.

True enough, the dog slinked closer, ears flopped over, and nudged Ben's leg with his snout. Happy to oblige—he liked dogs, and he didn't want this one to attack him while he was nibbling on its mom's neck— Ben dropped his hand on the dog's head and scratched his ears.

"Nash. Go lay down." Carlie, still pressed middle to middle with Ben, told the dog. "Mommy's busy."

The dog nudged Carlie's leg and then trotted off and disappeared through the doorway. Ben drew back and narrowed his eyes at her.

"Do you do this often?"

Rather than be angry or offended, Carlie dropped her head back and laughed. The look on her face was pure amusement, pure happiness. Again, he told himself he should walk away. He'd already ruined Heather's life. No need to do the same with another sweet girl just because he was attracted to her.

"No." She combed her fingers up through the back of his short, cropped hair. The touch sent a shiver of pleasure through him. "I didn't think it would work."

Ben laughed softly and shook his head.

"What?" She moved again, this time to draw her other hand back and flatten it on his chest.

"You're adorable," he said softly. "Do you know that?"

"Then adore me," she whispered. "Don't keep me waiting."

"Jesus, Carlie," he hissed.

She drew her hands away from him now to unbutton her blouse. Her slow, deliberate movements drove him to the edge of sanity. Hungry for everything she was offering, Ben watched her elegant fingers work each button. She wore a dainty silver band on her right index finger. No other jewelry. Her bare nails were short and rounded. Ben closed his eyes for a moment, imagining her hands on his shoulders, digging in for purchase as he moved inside her.

"Now who's keeping who waiting?"

She grinned when she met his eyes. "Don't ruin this."

"What about—?" Dinner. He was going to ask about dinner, but the word vanished from his tongue, from his mind, when Carlie parted her blouse and shrugged out of it.

"It can wait." She arched an eyebrow hopefully.

He lifted a trembling hand to her and stroked his fingertip over her breastbone.

"Are you sure?"

Carlie laughed softly and ducked her chin to her chest, but not before Ben saw her cheeks flush with color.

"This is the first time I've done this, and I'm feeling like it's not working."

"Done what exactly?" Ben dropped his hands and took a step back. No way was he going to take her virginity. He had no intention of sticking around. They could have a fun little fling, a little bit more than his typical one-night stands as of late. But that was it. If Carlie was a virgin, she might see everything differently once they had sex.

"Oh, for God's sake, Ben." She rolled her eyes. "I'm not a virgin. I meant it's my first time trying to seduce someone." She laughed and shook her head, obviously embarrassed. "I promise I lost my virginity when I was nineteen."

"You're trying to seduce me?" His turn to tip his head and waggle his brows at her.

"I suck at it, huh?'

"You most certainly don't," he answered. "You had me roped in from the word go."

"You wanted to sleep with me when—"

Horrified by what she was about to say, Ben lifted his hand and laid his finger over her lips.

"No. Something about you got under my skin, yes," he admitted. He trailed his fingers down her bare belly and hooked them in the waistband of her jeans. "But I don't think those kinds of thoughts when I'm working, Carlie."

Eyes locked with his, she nodded. "I know."

"I wanted to kiss you the first time I saw you at Beanstalks."

"And when did you decide you wanted to sleep with me?"

"About two seconds after I decided I wanted to kiss you."

"And yet, we're still standing here." She shrugged, her lips tipping into a tiny little smirk, all but daring him to strip her and take her on the floor.

"We don't have to rush it," he told her.

"Say that again." She sashayed her hips just a bit, just a bit too far from his middle for him to feel the movement. His dick throbbed with need.

"That we don't have to rush?"

"I like the sound of that." She reached behind her and suddenly the elastic in her bra was loose and the lace cups slipped low on her breasts. "Most guys I've been with are always in a rush to the finish line."

"She says as she continues to undress in front of me."

Carlie laughed again.

"I love your laugh," he told her.

"I love your smile," she answered immediately. "You should do it more often."

"Carlie, are you sure about this?"

Instead of answering him, Carlie tugged the white lace, slipped the straps over her arms, and dropped her bra on the floor. Ben moved quickly to pick her up and throw her over his shoulder.

"Seriously?"

Her giggle did something to him. Not his dick— thank God, because much more, and he was going to come in his jeans. No, the giggle poked at him, much higher. Right in the heart. He liked it. He wanted to hear more of it. More laughter. More sighing with pleasure.

"I take my clothes off, and you throw me over your shoulder—"

"Ever hear of a fireman's carry?" He swatted her butt. "Which way's your bedroom?"

"Wow, Ben." She moaned softly. "That made me wet."

"Bedroom," he grunted. "Or I'm gonna put you down right here on the floor and make love to you."

"I don't mind the sound of that."

"Yeah? You wanna do it right here? What about rugburn?"

"Could be worth it."

Ben laughed and shook his head. "If I promise to bring you right back here later and give you rugburn, will you tell me where your bedroom is?"

"Through that doorway and to the left."

Once he was through the doorway, he saw the lamp-light in her bedroom. Had she been expecting this? Or did she always leave her light on in the evening? Her bed wasn't made, but it wasn't turned down, either, as if in anticipation of a sexy night.

He tossed her gently to her bed and looked his fill when she raised her arms over her head.

"Ben?"

It took every bit of his strength to drag his gaze from her bare breasts. When he saw her sink her teeth into her lower lip, he groaned again and tugged his shirt off over his head.

"Oh God." Carlie propped herself up on her elbows, her eyes trekking over his bare chest and abdomen. "You're beautiful."

"That's my line," he told her. He took his wallet from his pocket and set it on the little metal nightstand by her bed. He had come prepared, and he wanted the condoms handy when it was time. "I want you naked."

His chest ached as he watched her lie back again, her fingers on the button of her jeans.

"Nope." He shook his head. "I wanna do it."

Ben propped his knee on the bed and leaned over her. His fingers brushed hers as he worked her jeans open and unzipped them. He took a moment to admire her flat belly, the skin in the v of her open zipper, the white lace of her panties just visible there.

Hungry for a taste of her belly, Ben dipped his head closer and pressed his open mouth to her hot skin. Carlie gasped and jumped, but before he could pull away from her, she cupped the back of his head in her hand.

"You like that?" He nipped at her skin hard enough to leave a mark, but she only moaned softly and parted her legs for him. Ben looked up at her as he backed over her, dropping sweet kisses as he moved. At the open v of her jeans, he tugged at her lace panties with his teeth.

"More," she whispered, her hand still cupped around his head.

Ben tipped his head up enough to see the heat in her face. Blowing over her exposed panties, he nudged her thighs open further with his hand.

"Ben."

"Touch yourself," he told her.

"I want you to." She rolled her head on the bed, her face twisted in agony now. Ben rubbed his hand over her core, the denim and her panties still between them. "Ohmygod."

"Touch your nipples."

Carlie did as he asked, one hand smoothing up over her breasts. He watched, his heartbeat pounding in his throat, as she rolled a nipple between her thumb and forefinger.

"Do you touch yourself, Carlie?"

"Yes."

"Can you get yourself off?"

"Yes."

As he talked, he continued to rub the denim between her legs. Carlie lifted her hips, face still a mask of need.

"Ben, please."

"Are you wet? For me?"

"Yes."

"Do you want me to kiss you there?"

She tightened her grip on the back of his head and pinched her nipple hard. Ben felt her stomach muscles tighten as she moaned softly and chanted his name.

"Carlie?"

"Hmm?" Head on the bed, she parted her lips and panted to catch her breath.

"Are you ready now?"

"Ready for what?"

"The real deal." He unwound her hand from around his head and licked her palm.

"Ben." Still panting, she lifted her head to look at him.

"Can you come again?"

She laughed softly. "I have no idea."

"How do you have no idea?"

"No guy's ever been worried about it before."

"Well." Ben raised up on his knees and offered her a grin. "I'm gonna worry about it, Carlie. I'm gonna make you come so hard you forget anyone else who's ever been inside you."

# CHAPTER
# NINETEEN

Carlie tried to swallow as she watched Ben ease backwards from the bed. Mouth dry, she simply stared at him, wide-eyed, waiting. Hoping he delivered as promised. It was true what she said. She wasn't a virgin, but she wasn't swimming in experience, either. And the guys she had been with were *already* forgettable compared to Ben Sager.

Something told her she would do well to keep that to herself.

"Speechless?" he asked with a sly grin.

"Maybe," she admitted.

She propped herself on her elbows again and tracked the movement of the muscles under his skin as he moved again to put a knee on the bed and reached for her hips.

"Bend your knees," he instructed her. When she did, he tugged at the denim and inched it down. Desperate for his eyes on her, his hands and mouth on her, she lifted her hips so he could slide her jeans off. He tossed them aside, greedy eyes drinking her in.

Carlie squirmed on her bed when Ben smoothed his hands from her knees down her inner thighs. Her belly flip-flopped, skin burning with anticipation, with need, when he jerked his gaze up to hers and pressed his thumb to her clit. Desperate to be rid of the barrier between them, she hooked her thumbs in her panties and pushed at them. Her frantic moves brought a devilish grin to his face, but he didn't help her.

To her dismay, he trailed his fingers up her thighs and lifted her right foot.

"What are you doing?" She wailed—half giggle, half pout.

"You asked me to adore you, Carlie Beringer." He kissed the arch of her foot. "So, I'm going to adore every inch of your beautiful body."

She gasped softly when he pressed his thumb into the arch of the same foot and rubbed a small circle.

"You could do all of that later," she whispered.

"Who would've thought you would be so greedy in bed?"

The amused grin on his face should have embarrassed her, but the heat rushing her body was all arousal.

"Ben, I've dreamt of you inside me."

"I'm gonna be inside you, Carlie." His growl lit every nerve in her body on fire.

Carlie closed her eyes as he kissed a path from her foot to her knee and then started the same treatment on her other foot and leg. Part of her was acutely aware that she'd been topless for a long time now, and he hadn't touched her breasts. Her nipples tightened at the thought, but his warm velvet tongue painting her thigh, his gentle love bites that would bruise her, mark her as his, paralyzed her.

"Turn over."

Too lost in the pleasure of his kisses, the alternate licking and sucking on her skin—no one had ever kissed her like this, so how could she have known what it would be like for a man to devour her this way?—she turned over to her belly and moaned with pleasure when Ben trailed his fingertips back down her legs to her feet.

Again, he kissed and rubbed her arches. His tongue hot and wet on her ankles and then the backs of her knees. Carlie wiggled under him, loving his attention and still needing more.

"Am I hurting you?" he asked as he eased his weight down on her. He dropped a wet kiss between her shoulder blades.

"Scarring me for any other man," she mumbled with a lazy smile. "Desperately hurting my nipples and—"

"How am I hurting your nipples?" He nudged her hair from her neck. The little nibbles and the flick of his tongue over her hot skin drew shivers. Again, he sounded amused, and Carlie thrilled at the knowledge that she could make him laugh.

"They would really like for you to touch them," she answered.

"I'll get there." He licked a path from her neck to the center of her back. "And when I do? They *are* going to hurt."

"I can't wait," she whispered.

"And another thing?" Ben shifted his weight, his thick cock pressing deliciously on her butt.

"Hmm?"

"When we're in bed together? No talking about other guys. You're mine, Carlie."

She bit her lip and nodded. If she poured out her thoughts right now, Ben Sager would be the one to run from what was happening between them. He might be all in for a fling. Earth-shattering sex, if his foreplay was any indication. But Carlie knew he had no intention of sticking around. Feeling anything for her beyond lust. Maybe he was protective of her because of how they met. But Ben Sager wasn't looking for love.

He sure as hell didn't need to know she was.

"Say it." He rocked forward, pressing her harder into the mattress. "Say you're mine."

"I'm yours, Ben." She lifted her head and peeked at him over her shoulder. "Take me."

"Is your back okay?"

Carlie tensed. That's what he meant when he asked if he was hurting her. He was worried about her injuries from the accident. She didn't want to be reminded of that, of those moments when she was completely undone and vulnerable. When Ben had seen her that way. She knew that was probably what made him see her as a kid.

"It's fine," she assured him.

"Have you had sex since the accident?"

"Is that a trick question?"

"What?" He inched backward, straddling her hips, and hooked his fingers in her panties.

"You just told me no talking about other guys."

"So, you have had sex since then? Did it hurt?"

"I haven't, Ben," she told him. "Please just touch me. I'm fine."

He didn't respond. Instead, she felt him tug her panties down a bit, exposing the top of her butt cheeks.

"You are definitely fine," he murmured, his fingers grazing her skin.

"I'm so wet for you, Ben," she confessed. "You're killing me."

"Tell me what you want."

"You know what I want."

"Tell me. Every little thing you want me to do."

"Make me come."

Heavy, hot hands gripped her hips and without warning, he sunk his thumbs into her cheeks and spread her open.

"Every little thing, Carlie. Tell me."

"Touch me."

"Where?"

"Put your fingers inside me, Ben. Please."

Carlie closed her eyes as Ben pulled her panties to the side and rubbed his fingers through her wet folds. She still wanted to be naked. To turn over and feel his hands, his mouth, on her breasts. But this—his fingers between her legs and his eyes on her when she couldn't see him was something new. Something a little bit frightening and so sexy, she knew she would explode, and it would be over again, all too fast.

She pushed her middle off the bed when he eased a finger inside her, working with him to find the angle she wanted. Both hands on her, he pushed a second finger deep inside her and pressed her clit.

"Ben," she sobbed as she rocked backwards on his hands, the sheet on her nipples an added pleasure.

"Come for me, Carlie." His voice low and tight, he scissored his fingers inside her and added pressure to her clit.

"It's too fast." Embarrassed to lose control so quickly, and embarrassed to be sobbing with need, she buried her face in her comforter.

"Sweetheart, we'll do it again," he promised her.

That did it. The *sweetheart* thing. She shattered, wave after wave of heat and pleasure climbing from her toes to her fingertips.

"I'm gonna make you come again and again and again."

"Ben," she whispered. "Oh God. I'm quivering. Stop."

"Too much?"

He shifted behind her, but he stroked her slowly, drawing out her release. Carlie collapsed, boneless and panting. Tears wet her face. What would he think? Did other women come so hard they teared up? Something told her Ben Sager had been with a lot of women, not just the ex-wife he still bought presents for.

Carlie bent her legs and curled up on her side when Ben moved, when he eased his fingers from her and gently pulled away. She watched with one eye as he scooted up the bed to lay beside her.

"I'm sorry," she whispered.

"Don't apologize." He kissed her cheek. "When you come like that, I feel like a fucking king."

Carlie lifted a hand, pressed her fingertips to his cheek.

"Not a king." She shook her head. "Kings are fat and fussy."

The loud roar of laughter and the way the skin around his eyes crinkled with mirth made Carlie's heart sing.

"A warrior then. Does that work for you?" He arched his eyebrows.

"Yes."

He rubbed his lips over hers, and she thrilled at the feel of their skin, their heat together.

"I've been thinking about you. Like this."

"Do you touch yourself when you think about me?"

"You know I do," she said with a soft laugh.

"And does it feel like that did?"

"No."

Carlie watched him lick his fingers, the same fingers he had pushed inside her.

"Ready for more?" He trailed the same fingers over her neck and the slope of her breast to finally tweak her nipple.

"Yes."

"What do you wanna do now?" That grin again. Carlie laughed and lifted her head to kiss him. "I wanna rip those sexy little panties off you and spread your legs open and taste you."

"I want that, too." She nodded and slipped her arms around his shoulders as he eased over on top of her.

"I want to play with your nipples." He flicked her upper lip with his tongue.

"Me too," she agreed with a lazy grin.

"I wanna bury my cock inside you and feel all that slippery wet heat squeeze me."

Breathless again, Carlie licked her lips.

"I want that." She swallowed hard as she smoothed her hands over his back. She molded the hard muscles with her palms, reveling in the sweat and heat on his skin. Being with her like this made him hot and sweaty. Made his cock feel like steel, pressed to her middle. Carlie loved that he responded that way to her touch, to her nudity.

"Now?" He pinched her nipple hard enough to make her jump.

"Yes."

She watched his fingers play with her nipple for a moment before sliding over her belly and dipping below her panties and between her legs. Before she could process the feeling, he moved again, but when he fingered the button on his jeans, he kissed her. Carlie met his lips, his tongue, with the same hungry greed. Desperate to feel him inside her, but unwilling to let this kiss end, she cupped his cheek in her hand to hold him there.

"Ben," she breathed his name when he did finally break the kiss. She licked her lips and watched him crawl backwards to stand. She lowered her gaze to his hands at his zipper and watched with her heart in her throat as he eased his jeans down. The bulge in his gray boxer briefs thrilled her. She reached for her panties.

"Uh-uh." He clucked his tongue as he kicked his jeans off. "That's my job."

"Then let me do you." She scooted over the bed to be

close to him. Heat rolled off his skin when she pressed her open mouth to his flat, washboard stomach.

"I've thought about you on your knees with your mouth on me," he admitted. Carlie looked up at him and reached for the waistband of his boxers. "But we're saving that for later."

"Let me see you."

"If you get your tongue anywhere near my dick, I'm gonna come," he told her. "And I wanna come inside you right now."

"Promise." She nodded.

He laughed again.

"You promise you're gonna be good?" He tipped his head. "Or that you're gonna put your mouth on me?"

"Don't I owe you one?"

Ben cupped her chin in his hand and forced her to look at him.

"Don't." He pressed her lip with his thumb. "If you wanna put your mouth on me, hell yes, I want that. But don't ever think I expect it."

"Ben, I wanna taste all of you," she whispered. "This is a body women only get to play with in their wildest fantasies."

"And I will indulge your every fantasy," he promised. He gave her a gentle push so she would fall back to the bed. "After we make love."

Carlie raised her brows expectantly, but rather than shuck his own boxer briefs, Ben leaned over the bed to remove her panties. Eyes locked with his, she lifted her hips again, and this time, Ben slipped the lacy scrap down her legs and tossed it on the floor.

"Let me look."

The command shot a thrill through her. She drew her knees up and spread her legs.

"I *will* taste that pretty pussy," he told her.

"I want your mouth on me."

She watched him reach for his wallet and pluck a small handful of condoms from inside.

"I'm afraid to ask," she said with a grin.

"I'm always prepared," he told her, "but the extras are special for you."

Afraid she would say something wrong—something about feelings, other than the sexy, hot, wet kind—and scare him off, Carlie simply pressed her lips together and waited. She gasped out loud when Ben finally shoved his underwear down. His cock sprung free, thick and ready to play.

"Last chance to run." He picked up a condom and watched her expectantly.

"Make love to me, Ben."

She might have felt anxious about using those words. Because Carlie knew this was just sex. Maybe friendship. But Ben Sager wasn't going to love her. And yet, he had been the one to call what they were doing here making love. Twice.

Heat roared through her body as he tore the condom wrapper open with his teeth and tossed it aside. She watched, greedy for what was coming but also just the sight of his fingers rolling the rubber over his thick cock, the drop of moisture already there on his head.

She reached for him when he was ready, when he put a knee on the mattress between her legs. Arms around his shoulders, she welcomed his body as he settled between her thighs. His mouth found hers for a deep, wet kiss as he eased the tip of his cock inside her.

"Perfect." He dipped his head to the hollow between her face and her shoulder and sunk his teeth into her skin as he drove deep inside her.

Carlie wound her legs around his hips and locked her ankles, knowing she would never want to let him go.

# TWENTY

"Do we need to talk about this?"

Carlie moaned softly and stretched her arms up over her head. Ben dropped his gaze to admire the view of her naked breasts. He wanted to suckle her again, but she was probably already sore. While Carlie hadn't been a shy virgin, Ben assumed she didn't invite too many men into her bed, either. He had been careful with her at first, worried about her back and her legs—the image of her broken and bleeding in his head at the worst of times.

To his delight, Carlie Beringer was enthusiastic in bed and more than willing to try and do anything. They had burned through two of the four condoms already, and in between times, Ben had planted himself between her legs and licked her to more than one orgasm.

No doubt she would be sore tomorrow. That knowledge—knowing that he was the one to deliver overwhelming pleasure for her—puffed him up a bit and made him feel like a warrior. That thought made him chuckle; he would be her warrior if she wasn't into kings.

"Dinner?" she asked. Head buried in her pillow, and her hair spread out around her, she licked her lips and stared up at him. "You didn't like spaghetti in bed?"

"I loved spaghetti in bed," he promised her. He curved his fingers around her breast but forced himself not to touch her nipple. The bites and the sucking would take their toll and leave her chapped. "That's not what I'm talking about."

"I've never had spaghetti in bed."

Her impish grin touched him. What was it about this woman that could make him happy? All she had to do was smile at him, and his heart got all soupy and drippy. She made him forget things. No, that wasn't true. Ben knew that even after this incredible night with Carlie, he would eventually go back to his shithole apartment, and he would go to bed and lie awake thinking about Schafer. But something about that knowledge felt different. Usually, any thought of Schafer made his chest tight, like his ribs were contracting and squeezing his lungs until it was fucking impossible to draw a single breath.

Tonight, that pain, the grief, was there. But the joy of lying here with Carlie in his arms made it feel far away. Rather than the raging storm that dogged him since his partner died, the guilt was distant thunder. Just enough to remind him it was still there.

But bearable.

"Neither have I."

He and Heather had their share of crazy tales of sex

and items most people didn't associate with sex. But they had never eaten a spaghetti dinner in bed.

"I mean this." He leaned close to kiss Carlie's cheek. "Us."

"Carlie—"

"I get it, Ben," she assured him.

"Don't do that." He let his eyes roam her face, touched again by her youth, her innocence. "That makes me feel like a bastard who just wanted to get in your pants."

She stared at him without answering for a long moment. He might have worried about what she was thinking, but her face was the picture of serene. Finally, she rolled to her side to look at him. Ben closed his eyes for a moment when she pressed her fingers to his neck and then smoothed them up over the stubble on his cheek.

"I wanted you there." She shrugged. "I know there's still a part of you that thinks I'm a kid—"

Ben opened his mouth to argue with her, though hell if he knew what to say. Because she was right.

"I see it in the way you look at me," she continued. "Just remember I'm a big girl, and I wanted this, too."

"I'm not a good guy, Carlie." He moved enough to press his forehead to hers and locked gazes with her. "I don't want to hurt you. But I will."

"How?" She pressed a chaste kiss on his mouth. "Tell me how you're going to hurt me."

"Just." He shrugged. "I'm divorced. I've let my little girl down. I drink too much. I think too much. I—"

"Talk too much."

Her whisper cut him off.

"What?" He laughed softly and bit at her fingertip when she touched his lip.

"Can I tell you something?"

"What?" He braced himself. What in the world was she going to say? He hitched his shoulders and flopped back to lie flat on her bed. Maybe he should get dressed and head out. Maybe he had already overstayed his welcome.

"I like your laugh," she said simply.

"I still sleep with Heather." The words tumbled out before he could even think them.

"Like...you slept with her yesterday, and when you leave my bed, you're going to go home to her and sleep with her tonight?"

"How are you so calm about what I said?"

"Well, if you say yes to what I just asked, I might not be," she admitted.

Ben didn't want her jealousy. He didn't want Carlie to be clingy. He didn't want her to feel possessive of him, which was ridiculous, considering he demanded her to say she belonged to him.

But her admission sent a rush of relief through him. It stung to think she wouldn't care if he was still involved with his ex. Did she really want nothing more than a fling? Was it like Heather said? Hadn't Carlie herself said it? Women fantasized about playing with a body like his.

"I haven't been with her for a month, maybe. I dunno. The point is she divorced me because—we split up because I chased my demons in the wrong places. She might have waited forever for me to get my head figured out. But I left. Because it wasn't fair for me to do that to her."

"Horrible of you to be noble about it," Carlie mumbled. Ben lifted his head to peek at her.

"And then even after the divorce, I've used her."

"So. Here's the thing." Carlie propped her head on her hand and stared down at him. "You're giving yourself too much power."

"What do you mean?"

"I'm assuming Heather's an adult. And I assume she's intelligent and probably gorgeous. And capable of moving on. If she didn't want to sleep with you after the divorce, she wouldn't."

"I still drink too much."

"Maybe." Carlie shrugged. Ben wanted to squirm under her heavy gaze. "But you haven't around me."

At a loss for what to say again, how to warn her off when she didn't seem inclined to listen, Ben sighed.

"Look. I get it. You're telling me not to look at you with starry eyes and think this is going anywhere." She dragged her teeth over her lip. "Are you gonna hit me? If you get drunk one night? Is that part of the warning?"

"I've never hit a woman," he snapped.

"Well, then, I'm not worried," she answered simply. "And if I do look at you with stars in my eyes, and you don't wanna know what I'm thinking, that's my business. Isn't it?"

"Carlie—"

"You promise not to get drunk and mean with me, and I promise not to stalk you when you decide you're tired of me."

"So, we're making a—what? A business deal?"

Carlie snorted. "Why can't we just be friends?"

"You're a friends-with-benefits kind of girl?"

"No." She moved slowly, one hand flat on his chest, as she eased over to straddle him. "I'm not. I'm a hopeless romantic, Ben Sager. And I believe everyone has a soulmate out there somewhere. And yes, I am looking for mine."

Ben frowned up at her, uncomfortable with her talking about finding someone to love her while she sat atop him, nude and marked with his love bites.

"I thought we talked about this."

Unable to help himself, he reached for her breasts and rolled her nipples into a hard pinch.

"I'm not talking about anyone specific," she answered. "I'm just telling you what I'm looking for."

Ben clenched his teeth and closed his eyes as she inched backwards over him.

"I'm too old for you." He tangled his fingers in her hair and growled with satisfaction when she sank her teeth into his upper thigh.

"If you say so," she agreed.

"Carlie."

"You talk too much," she told him again. "Are you going to Heather's tonight?"

"I hadn't planned to leave your bed tonight."

"Then stop talking."

IT DROVE HIM TO DISTRACTION—THE carefree way Carlie had welcomed him into her bed and the pleasure she had taken from his kisses and his body and the way she refused to be afraid of him. Ben didn't want a relationship. Hell, he'd been there, done that. No need to do it again.

And yet, had he read Carlie wrong? Yes, that flicker of youth—the very same thing that had painted her young and vulnerable—was very evident in everything she did. Including the way she made love. But wasn't she going to demand he only see her? Wasn't she going to ask for more? Didn't she want him to feel something more than lust?

The hell of it was, he *did*. The mere thought of Carlie's pale flat belly and her soft sighs when he kissed her neck made him hard as steel. But there was more. *He* felt *more*, so how did *she not feel more*? Ben wanted to protect her, yes. He wanted to shield her from hurt, from bad things. Including himself. But there was more.

Ben wanted her laughter. He wanted her zest for life, but he wanted it aimed in his direction. No, he didn't want her to stalk him. But he wanted to share every day with her. Not just the nights they spent in her bed. He loved the sneak peek he got of her day-to-day life when he was at her place. He liked Nash. He loved watching Carlie frown and study a recipe, even as she apologized in advance of fixing him dinner, because she wasn't a cook. He loved watching *Chicago PD* with her and found it funny that she wasn't a fan of *Chicago Fire*. She made him coffee when he left her house in the mornings. She was always ready and hungry to make love before he left, but if he was in a hurry, she was happy to send him off with a kiss.

She was everything he didn't want, and it made him restless and angry that she seemed content with the easy, sexy things they did together.

Funny how she made him feel good. About everything. It didn't seem to matter what sort of day he was having; he would hear a slice of dialogue walking through the common room in the firehouse or something on TV and think of Carlie. Bozeman talking about his wife and kids ambushing him in a snowball fight—suddenly Ben wanted to take Carlie and Naomi to the park and make snow angels and a snowman. Car commercials on TV reminded him of kissing Carlie the first time in the parking lot and then leaning into her window to kiss her again. Right before trying to chase her off.

Music made him think about her, and it wasn't only country music. Carlie had something playing all the time when he was at her place, usually classic rock. He wasn't much of a dancer, but one night, she had a sexy Joe Cocker song playing, and she'd pressed up against him in the kitchen and draped her arms over his shoulders, and the next thing he knew they were dirty dancing and then they were naked and living out Ben's first fantasy about her right there on her kitchen table.

She owned him. He had a feeling she knew it, and maybe that's why she didn't push him to make promises. Carlie asked about Naomi often enough, but she never pushed him about spending time with her, either.

"What're you thinking?"

Standing between her legs, Ben ducked his head to her chest and sighed. Half of him wanted to broach the subject—introducing Carlie to his little girl. Half of him still wanted to drop a kiss on the top of Carlie's head, pat her shoulder, and tell her it had been fun. They'd been sleeping together long enough that he should be bored and ready to move on. It made his head hurt that he didn't want to. At least Heather had let up on him about it. Then again, that was probably because he hadn't spent any time at all around his ex-wife. When it was his time to be with Naomi, he had been picking her up and making small talk with Heather and leaving the house. He and Naomi had done the park thing—tossed a few snowballs and made snow angels. He had treated her to hot cocoa. They'd seen the latest animated movie, but Naomi still had trouble sitting still for too long at a time.

That's what he felt like now. Restless and antsy like he had to move. To do something different. And the only thing in his life that he could do different was Carlie.

"Why don't you ever ask me about Naomi?" He spoke without lifting his head. Her sweatshirt smelled fresh, recently laundered, and he liked the warmth in the skin of her neck.

"I ask about Naomi all the time," she reminded him.

Ben closed his eyes as she smoothed her fingers over his head, through his short hair.

"I mean meeting her. Why don't you want to meet her?"

When his question was meet with silence, Ben huffed a sigh and finally looked up to find her watching him closely.

"I…" She sighed and shrugged. "I guess I figured you wouldn't want me around her."

"Why's that?"

"Well, because we're just…messing around, and we have no future together, and so you wouldn't want her to…"

Ben nodded. Of course, she was right. Not a good idea to bring women around Naomi. Not until she was much older and could understand that her dad wasn't looking to ever settle down again.

"Is that what this is for you?"

The words were out of his mouth before he realized he was going to speak. Why was he pushing this? If Carlie was okay with a casual affair, why was he pushing her to admit she wanted more?

Carlie frowned and nodded as she looked around his kitchen. He'd dragged her here a few weeks ago thinking that would be when she would cut and run. Seeing the tiny little apartment he was living in as a grown man. Seeing the sad, gloomy living conditions might drive it home for her that they had no future.

That plan had backfired when Carlie brought her usual sunshine to his place. Even the first night, her laughter filled the rooms, and they'd shared peanut butter crackers in this very kitchen, and they'd made love in the bed he hadn't made in God only knows how long. When she was gone, the next day, damned if he didn't notice the way the sunlight crept over the living room a bit at a time and lit the cozy little space.

"Ben, I don't—"

His door banged open so suddenly they both jumped.

Ben swung his gaze around, shocked to see his ex-wife walk in.

"I need to talk to you."

Still stunned, Ben blinked at her for a moment, wondering why she hadn't knocked. And why he hadn't asked her that, and what it must look like to Carlie.

Even though it didn't matter because they were having a casual affair.

"Heather."

"Ben." She sighed as she looked at Carlie, clearly giving her the once-over.

"Kinda busy," Ben told her.

"She might want to hear this, too." Heather swallowed hard and finally moved into the kitchen with them.

"Where's Naomi?"

"At my parents' house." Heather waved his concern away. "I had a doctor's appointment this morning, Ben."

"I should go." Carlie jumped down from the counter. Her flat, toneless voice was like a sucker punch to his gut. Here he had been goading her, trying to—what? Make her admit that she had feelings for him? Just so he could push her away and not deal with those feelings? With his own feelings?

Is that what the problem was? Was he *scared* of what he was feeling for Carlie?

He'd been goading her, ready to jump on her if she said something that made him feel threatened, and now Heather had stormed in and stolen the stage. And done what he hadn't been able to do.

Carlie was upset. Whether that meant angry or

jealous or hurt, he didn't know. But she pushed by him to grab her coat and avoided his eyes.

"I'm pregnant," Heather announced.

Worried about Carlie, worried about her leaving when she was upset and driving home alone, it took a few moments for Heather's words to sink in. When they did, they were heavy on his shoulders, heavy enough to drive him to his knees.

"Pregnant?" he repeated. Ben jerked his gaze away from Carlie to look at his ex-wife.

# TWENTY-ONE

Carlie might have laughed. If she could breathe. Heather's words were a steel blade in her chest, right through her heart. Ben would never love her now. Not with another child on the way. He was a good man, trying hard to be bad, mean, maybe because he didn't like himself. Carlie had loved him every way she could without saying so. She'd kissed him, head to toe. She'd held him when he slept. She'd given him her complete trust and let him inside her body, slept in his arms, night after night. And still, he hadn't confided in her about what had broken him. He didn't whisper things about loving her. He never referenced a future.

She had kidded herself. Believed she could be the kind of girl to live and love in the moment. How unfortunate to learn she was wrong, to have her house of cards fall down around her with an audience. It was bad enough that Ben would see she was upset. Carlie didn't know Heather, not other than the things Ben had told her about his ex-wife. Ben still cared about her, so that said something about who she was as a woman.

But that didn't mean Carlie wanted to fall apart while she watched.

She pulled her coat from the chair wondering if they were still sleeping together. Surely, he wouldn't have done that to either of them, would he? He'd warned her from the very beginning that he wasn't a good guy, but all evidence to the contrary had made Carlie shrug that warning off.

It didn't bother her that Ben and Heather had been together after their divorce. That wasn't her business. But if Ben was warming Heather's bed, making love to Heather in the times that he wasn't with Carlie, that was different. She wouldn't forgive that.

Not that it mattered.

Because they had talked about it and agreed to keep it casual.

Too bad her heart hadn't listened.

"Please don't go."

Startled by Heather's plea, Carlie looked up to find Ben's ex-wife watching her closely.

"I'm sorry. I shouldn't have done it this way, but I've been carrying this around for a few days, and I'm sick about it. I don't know what to do. I don't know what the answer is." Heather frowned and turned her attention back to Ben. "I was afraid to tell you. I finally got up the nerve to come."

She tossed her hands up helplessly and licked her lips.

"I've tried three other times, Ben," she confessed.

"But you just went to the doctor today."

Carlie eyed Ben silently. His clenched jaw looked carved of stone. Fire burned in his eyes, but Carlie knew it wasn't lust. Not this time.

"I did a home test a few weeks ago," Heather whispered. "It was positive. But I kept hoping for a false positive."

"And it's mine?"

Carlie dipped her head as a rush of heat flamed over her face. She felt embarrassed to be here, to witness this conversation. Even if Heather had just needed to come here and tell Ben, just blurt it out, she could have waited until Carlie was gone.

A choked little sob drew Carlie's attention again. She met Heather's eyes and steeled herself for the woman to go on the offensive.

"Yes, Ben, this is your baby." She might have answered Ben, but she stared at Carlie as she spoke.

"I really should—"

"I was afraid to tell you, because I know you're seeing...someone else now."

Carlie bit her lip. Ben was a new experience for her. That soulmate connection she'd felt when he held her gaze and talked her through the rescue. The wild attraction she had felt for him when they bumped into each other in Beanstalks. The crazy, adventurous sex, the way he focused on her pleasure with every move he made in her bed, and the way he held her and touched her with love.

Love he wouldn't vocalize.

Love that maybe she'd only imagined.

"Go." Carlie cleared her throat and finally looked Ben in the eyes. "I should go, Ben."

"I don't want you to."

Carlie tipped her head and narrowed her eyes at him.

"I don't think it's about what you want right now," she said quietly.

Heather's gaze burned a hole in her back, and Ben stared at her so intensely, she could feel his eyes searching her soul. On trembling knees, she reached for her keys on the table, grabbed her purse, and walked out of the room without another word.

Neither of them tried again to stop her, but Carlie's shoulders were frozen under their heavy stares. The tension in Ben's apartment was thick, and she imagined trying to fight her way to the door like a fireman walking through a smoke-filled room. Ben. In an apartment building like this. Full turn-out gear. Calling out for anyone stranded in the flames that devoured the walls around him.

She should have kissed him goodbye.

Outside, the night was brisk and dark. Carlie skipped down the steps to the sidewalk and eyed the four-wheel drive SUV parked behind her at the curb. Had to be Heather's. She saw the car seat in the back when she hurried between the vehicles to get to her door.

She should have kissed him. Because Carlie was certain this was the last she would see of Ben Sager.

She drove home in silence, too numb to want music. She'd known this day would come. Of course, she and Ben Sager weren't going to last. He was hung up on their age difference. On the fact that he was divorced, and she was *innocent*—his word, not hers. She'd known it would hurt, too. You don't invest yourself in a relationship with someone—even a casual relationship like Ben wanted—without feeling the shock, the pain, when it was over.

But she hadn't seen this coming. Ben's ex-wife pregnant. Carlie had no idea when that baby was conceived, but she did know Heather Sager was still in love with Ben. One look at the woman had said as much. No wringing her hands and openly sobbing. Nope. Heather Sager had been a woman desperate to hold herself together, to go easy on the man she loved.

After barging into his home and interrupting him with a new woman and announcing that she was pregnant.

Carlie could picture her face now as she drove. Glassy eyes, but other than that, she looked almost stoic. There hadn't been hatred in her gaze when she looked at Carlie. Not hatred, but defeat. Maybe a hint of apology, Carlie couldn't be sure.

Whatever the case, Ben had been in the middle of trying to drive Carlie off yet again. She wasn't sure why he pushed her that way now and then, trying to goad her into saying something so he could get angry. She wasn't sure if he knew he was so easily seen, if he knew Carlie was aware of what he was trying to do. He wouldn't scare her off. If they were going to end things, then Ben simply just had to say he was ready to move on.

Except not now.

Carlie sighed and curled her fingers around the bottom of the steering wheel. Ben's apartment was on the south end of town, her rental home on the north end.

Way too much thinking time tonight. At the stoplight on Broadway, the main road dividing the town into east and west, she flashed on the accident that brought Ben into her life. The raging beat of her heart when she saw the big truck coming straight at her. The way she'd fought through layers of darkness to open her eyes and find Ben looking at her through her window.

He'd prayed with her. She forgot to say her prayers most days, and she'd never made religion a priority. But in that moment, she had needed comfort, and Ben had given it to her.

Chilled now from the memories—as hazy as they were—Carlie leaned wearily over the steering wheel as she made her way home. Maybe he had been put in her life for a reason, and now it was time for them to move on.

At her house, she hurried inside to get Nash, as she thought about that saying—people in your life for a reason, some for a season. It sounded so noble, so mature. Nash dragged her down the block a bit, so she settled in for a short walk. At least to the corner.

It was crap—that saying about reasons and seasons. Someone had put Ben in her life, and once there, Ben had made himself at home. Ben had made her love him. And now he was uncomfortable with her, even when she hadn't hit him with any expectations or demands. Add in an ex-wife who still loved him and a child and another on the way, and Carlie suddenly looked like a naïve kid who didn't matter a bit in the big scheme of things.

That stung.

At the corner, she turned Nash back toward the

house and waited for him to finish his business. Once inside, she left her purse on the table and refused to look at her phone. She wanted to call Erin, but she would wait. Not just because she needed the time alone to sulk, to hurt, but because damned if she wanted a peek at her phone now.

She wasn't sure what would be worse—if Ben tried to call. Or if he didn't.

# CHAPTER
# TWENTY-TWO

Angry, restless, and ready to climb the walls, Ben huffed again, grumbled, and finally tore his eyes away from the door Carlie had quietly closed when she left. Heather sniffled—she hadn't cried until the door closed, and they were alone.

"Sit down."

At his command, she jerked her chin up to meet his eyes, but she didn't move.

"I don't wanna sit down."

"Christ, this is a mess." He folded his arms over his chest and stared at her, wishing Heather away. Wishing Carlie back.

"She's pretty," Heather said softly.

"How far along are you?"

"Are you gonna blame me for this?"

He dropped into the chair Carlie's coat had hung on just minutes ago.

"How can I blame you?" He tipped his head back and squeezed his eyes closed. "I was there, too."

"Do you want me to—"

"Don't." He pushed the word out through clenched teeth. "You know I would never ask you to abort a baby."

"I'm sorry, Ben," she whispered. "I didn't mean to come in here and blow things up. "

She moved now to join him at the table.

"It's fine."

"It's not." She tucked her hair behind her ear and then covered her eyes with her hand. "I just needed to talk about it. To tell you. I've come by so many times, so psyched and ready to just get it over with."

Ben pulled in a deep breath. Kept his gaze on the table.

"Either you're not here, or she is, and you're not alone."

"How far along?" he asked again.

"Fourteen weeks," she answered. "How long have you been in love with her?"

"I'm not," he snapped. He felt her eyes on him as he shoved the chair away to stand. "We're just friends."

"Right."

He bristled at Heather's sarcasm.

"The sex is incredible," he admitted. "But I told her from the beginning it couldn't be more."

"Well, you didn't get your memo, because it's more, Ben."

"What?" He stood with his back to her, but now, he looked at her over his shoulder. "What does that mean?"

"Well, first of all, you called this a mess. You're a stand-up guy, so you're going to be around for this baby—"

"Of course, I'm gonna be there for the baby. For you—"

"It's only a mess if you have feelings for her."

Ben flinched. Fuck all, Heather was right. If Carlie didn't mean anything to him, he would be okay with letting this be the end. He might call her in a day or two and say something hokey, something to give them closure. He hated that buzzword, but he wasn't such a dick that he would just let her hang until she figured it out on her own.

In reality, he was torn right now, needing to offer Heather comfort. A shoulder. Conversation. A promise that he would, indeed, be part of the baby's life, just as he was involved with Naomi. And wanting to follow Carlie. To promise her this, the baby, didn't have to change anything between them.

Except it did. No matter how he looked at it, it changed everything. Carlie was at home right now with Nash, thinking about him and Heather making a baby. Wondering if he had played her for a fool, if he had been sleeping with Heather all along. Maybe even assuming he and Heather would reconcile.

Hurting Carlie was the last damned thing he had ever wanted to do. And now he'd done it. He had known in the beginning that things between them would end in flames. Once again, he hadn't tried hard enough to save her, to push her away and keep her safe from his self-ishness.

"Ben, why can't you just admit you do?"

"Do what?"

Exhausted, he scrubbed his hands over his head and groaned, tempted to cut loose and yell his anger out.

"Have feelings for her."

"I'm ten years older than she is." He dropped into his chair again and met Heather's eyes. "I'm divorced. And it's my fault. I hurt you. I'm a part time dad, and now I'm doing that again. Our kids deserve better—"

"And?" Heather shrugged.

"Carlie is—is—she's got the world in front of her. She's a travel agent, Heather. She's been halfway around the world, and she should finish the other half. She should drink French wine in Paris with a French lover, and she should climb Kilimanjaro—"

"Is that what she wants?"

Ben drew back at Heather's interruption.

"Did she tell you that? She wants a French lover and adventures—"

"No." Ben shook his head and looked away. "She wants to find her soulmate. And she wants to watch *Chicago PD* with him. And she wants to go to the dog park on Saturdays and dance in the kitchen when she's trying to cook."

Heather's eyes filled again, but she nodded. "Has she done that with you?"

"It doesn't mean—"

"Ben." Heather leaned forward and reached for his hand. "Listen to me. Don't push her away. You're in love with her. And it sounds like she feels the same way. Stop being a martyr. You have to stop. It's okay to live. To love."

"You don't know what you're talking—"

"But I do," she whispered. "Because you did it to me first. I said till death do us part, and I meant every damned word."

Trapped by her honesty, Ben stood again and walked away from the table.

"And I still love you," Heather said to his back. "Too much to watch you do this to yourself again."

"I'm not good for her—"

"You're a good man, Ben," Heather argued. "And she would be lucky to have your love."

Ben cleared his throat, emotion making his chest ache.

"You're different with her," Heather continued.

"What does that mean?"

"You're happy," she said simply. "I don't see you much these days. But when I do, you're happy."

Ben blew out a deep breath and worked his mouth, trying to figure out what to say. How to say it. It had been such a damned long time since he'd been able to say the word love in that context. Other than telling Naomi he loved her, he couldn't remember the last time he'd said the word.

"And what if she doesn't feel that way? About me?" His voice was gruff with that emotion he tried so hard to bury. "Jesus, Heather, I can't talk to you about this."

"You do love her."

Heather stood. Ben watched her dig her keys from her pocket, only realizing now she wasn't wearing a coat.

"Where's your coat?" He stepped toward her and

rubbed his hands up and down her arms. "It's still cold out there."

Heather waved his concern away and shook her head.

"What if she does, Ben?" She stared at him boldly. "Are you willing to risk losing her?"

Something hurt a little bit in his chest, deep in his gut. Nerves. Fear. Chewing away at his insides. He recognized the fight or flight sensation—akin to what he felt when he assessed a fire before walking into the flames.

"You can always come back to me." Heather's sad smile tore at him. "Live half a life with me. Or you could go after her and have the life you really want."

PREGNANT.

Ben stewed over that word for several days. Part of him was thrilled. Being Naomi's dad was the best part of his life. But he had grown so comfortable with Carlie, he loved every moment they spent together, and that part of him worried about the pregnancy. And Heather. And what Carlie would think.

He gave her time to think. To remember that he had warned her, told her to run. But mostly, he took the time for himself because he was a coward.

Afraid to tell Carlie what he felt. Afraid she would laugh, that she was into him for the fun, for the here and now.

Afraid that she loved him. Because even after

Heather's absolution, Ben was still afraid he would hurt Carlie.

When he did go to her house, he held his breath, wondering if she would have company. Even if it was Erin. He couldn't walk into her place and be on display before her friends right now. Heather's pregnancy, and Carlie telling him it wasn't about what he wanted the night Heather made her announcement—all of it combined with the job, losing a young family to a trailer fire had dredged up the guilt over Shafer again—had chewed him up and left him raw.

Carlie's little car was in its spot. No cars parked close to it. Ben took a breath for courage, wished for a moment for a drink and then realized when he had Carlie, when he'd spent days and nights with Carlie, he hadn't needed liquid courage or the blissful numb that too much delivered. He closed his door quietly and made his way to her front door.

He didn't hear music, but Nash barked, alerting Carlie that someone was on her porch. She didn't come right away. Not until he rang the doorbell. She answered the door in a t-shirt he had left at her house. Faded blue —she said she liked it because it made his eyes pop, whatever that meant. Washed so many times, his old school logo was too worn to read. It hung long and loose over her yoga pants. Hair in a messy knot at the back of her head, she eyed him silently, waiting.

Ben cleared his throat and hung his head.

"Can I come in?"

She might not have heard him through the storm door. Without speaking, she pushed it open and stood frozen when he came inside. Nash greeted him with a soft woof and a nudge to his leg. Ben patted his head absently, eyes on Carlie.

"I have not been with her since we started seeing each other."

Ben wasn't sure where to start, and he was a little surprised when his mouth chose the subject of infidelity to begin.

Carlie closed the door and turned to him, but she still said nothing.

"She's...fourteen weeks," he continued to ramble. "And, um. She just needed to tell someone. No one knew, and it was—"

"You talk too much," Carlie said softly.

"Funny, because I don't know what the hell to say, Carlie."

She moved across the room and perched on the arm of her couch. The same couch they had spent hours on, watching TV, making out, sleeping.

"Here's the thing." She sighed and looked up at him with wide eyes. "You've been pushing me away since the first time we were together. Since the first time you kissed me."

"Carlie—"

"You were about to do the same the night..." She trailed off and shook her head. "I get it, Ben. Maybe you see me as naïve. Gullible. I don't know. But I'm not stupid. We had something really good, and now, for more than one reason, we should probably call it quits."

"What reasons?" He spoke so quietly, he barely heard himself.

"Well, you have a baby on the way. Your ex-wife is still in love with you. You made it clear to me from the beginning that we were just having fun—"

"How do you know she's still in love with me?"

Carlie sniffled and laughed softly. "I don't know. But it was obvious."

"Because Heather said it was obvious that there's something real between us."

"And if you need your ex-wife to point that out, that's a problem."

Ben groaned and paced across the room. Fingers looped around the back of his neck, he rolled his shoulders.

"I didn't want to feel this way, Carlie." He swallowed hard and clenched his teeth. "Because you deserve—"

"Don't."

Ben glanced at her over his shoulder when she interrupted him.

"Don't make excuses. We had a thing. It's done." She tossed her hands up and shrugged. "Does it hurt? Yes. Am I in love with you? Yes."

"Carlie."

"It's okay," she whispered and laughed. "I'm not gonna stalk you. I won't leave you threatening notes. I won't bother your wife or your kids."

"Carlie."

"I'll just love you a little less each day and maybe one day wake up and feel okay again."

"I don't want you to love me less each day."

"It's not about what you want," she said again.

"I lost a partner. In a housefire." He knuckled his

eyes, frustrated with the emotion. "And when the guilt got to me, I drank instead of letting Heather be there."

Carlie folded her arms over her chest.

"I'm afraid I'll do that to you. You make it better, Carlie, but what happens next time? Next time someone I love is hurt or injured? What then? What if your love isn't enough—"

"What if it is?" she asked quietly. "What if it is, Ben? What then?"

"I just." He groaned again. "I don't want to hurt you."

"Look." She stood and moved closer to him. "I can't forgive you for something you didn't do to me. I can't say it's okay. You have to do that for yourself. You have to let go of that guilt you're carrying around."

"He had twin girls."

Carlie flinched. Toe to toe with her, Ben saw the tears in her eyes.

"Here's the thing," she reached for him and smoothed her fingers over his chest, "When we were together, you laid that down. I saw it, Ben. I knew you were carrying something heavy, and I never asked because you didn't want me that close."

Ben took her hand in his and drew it to his mouth to kiss her knuckles.

"But I loved you every way you would let me without saying the words to make you run." The gentle pressure of her thumb on his lip made him ache.

"What if we try this, and we crash and burn, Carlie?" He turned her hand to kiss her palm.

"What if we try this, and we don't?" she argued.

"What if when we burn up, it's because we love each other, and we create that heat together?"

"I love you." His voice throbbed with his confession, his pledge. "I do. I love you, and that's why I'm so...I don't want to hurt you."

"If you love me, trust me," she said simply. "Trust me to love you. Trust me to have your back, Ben."

"Y ou sure about this?"

Despite the nerves threading through her belly right now, she was sure. Ben's invitation to join him and Naomi at the park this afternoon almost meant more to her than his love confession just a couple of weeks ago. *Almost.* Carlie suspected the words didn't come easy to a man like Ben Sager; he might feel everything deeply —love, grief, worry—but he wasn't the kind to gush about his feelings. Which meant if she were going to be with him, if she wanted him in her life, she had to trust that he loved her.

Asking her to meet Naomi and spend time with her was like Ben folding her into his arms at night and whispering in that gruff, almost harsh voice, that he loved her.

"Yes!" Carlie turned her head to look at him as he pulled his truck to the curb near the swing set at the park. The glimpse of Heather's vehicle in front of Ben's truck blew her nerves like she had swallowed a lit firecracker. She knew being with Ben, meeting Naomi, would mean more interaction with his ex-wife. Honestly, it scared the hell out of her, but she wouldn't admit that to him.

Rather than wait for Ben to open the door for her, she jumped out of the truck at the same time he did.

"Daddy!"

Carlie turned when she heard the squeals coming from the swing set. The little girl from Ben's pictures climbed from the swing, stumbling in her hurry to get to her daddy. Carlie felt a wave of nostalgia for her child-hood, her dad, but mostly, she was thrilled for Ben that Naomi loved him so much.

"Hey, Munchkin."

Carlie saw Ben drop to his knees as Naomi launched herself at him when she was within a few feet of him. Ben threw his arms around the little girl and squeezed her.

"Daddy." Naomi pulled back to look him in the eye as Ben stood. Her little legs wrapped around Ben's waist made Carlie ache a little inside. Would Ben want more children? She would be happy to have Naomi and the new baby in her life, but standing there watching her rugged and rough-around-the-edges man holding his daughter stirred a longing for children of her own.

"Naomi." Ben tipped his head and stared at his daughter. He looked so serious as he waited for Naomi to speak. Carlie held her breath, waiting for the moment his face would light up with a smile.

"There's grubs by the teeter-toddlers."

Carlie laughed softly. Ben had told her Naomi was a

fan of *The Three Billy Goats Gruff*, though the grubs scared her. She watched father and daughter now, rewarded by the beaming smile on Ben's face. Feeling like a thief stealing a special moment from Ben and Naomi, Carlie looked away and caught Heather's eyes. Ben's ex-wife approached slowly from the direction of the swing set. Her hair was pulled up in a no-nonsense ponytail, and she was dressed in plain jeans and a red t-shirt—as nonthreatening as she could be. And yet, she looked like a mom—a pretty cool mom—and that made Carlie's smile falter.

"Show me," Ben told Naomi. "I'll get rid of them."

"I suppose grubs are like trolls," Heather said as Ben headed toward the teeter-totters. He swung Naomi up and over his shoulders. The movement stole Carlie's breath, but Heather didn't flinch. It was obvious she trusted him with their daughter.

Carlie reluctantly drew her gaze from Ben again and glanced at Heather. Arms folded over her chest and the hint of a smile on her face, she turned to face Carlie.

"She loves the story, but it scares her," Heather announced. "She's afraid of a lot of things, but after she thinks about her fear long enough, she jumps to conquer it. Stories. Heights."

Carlie nodded. How was Heather standing there so calmly, telling her about the little girl she and Ben had made together?

"Before you guys got here," Heather continued, "she was on the jungle gym. On top of the jungle gym."

Carlie laughed softly.

"I'm Heather." Ben's wife took a deep breath, like she

was steeling herself for something. "I'm sorry. About barging in on you guys...dropping the bomb about the baby like I did."

"It's okay," Carlie said sincerely. "You and Ben have a long history together."

"I want you to know this happened before he found you." Heather touched her belly and glanced at Ben and Naomi again. "He's faithful. If he hurts you, it'll be the bottle. The job."

Carlie swallowed hard and nodded. "He's got a good heart."

Heather smiled, though Carlie saw her eyes fill with tears.

"He does," she agreed. "I'm not sure we'll be friends, Carlie. Or when it'll happen if it does."

Carlie stared at Heather silently, waiting for her to go on.

"Because I love him as much right this minute as I did when we were together."

"Mommy!" Naomi hollered. Her shrieks of laughter drew their attention. Ben sat on one side of a teeter-totter, close to the balancing bar, and Naomi sat on the other end. Carlie and Heather watched as Ben moved carefully, controlling the action so Naomi wouldn't get hurt.

"I want him to be happy," Heather said without looking at her. "You're good for him."

Carlie watched Heather make her way to Naomi. She gave the little girl a quick hug and kiss, touched Ben's shoulder, and then turned back toward Carlie. She passed Carlie silently and headed to her vehicle. If she had met Heather first, in some alternate life, Carlie thought they would be friends. She liked Ben's ex-wife. She also knew not to expect Heather to like her back.

She was watching when Ben gestured for her to join him and Naomi, so she crossed the park, passed the swings, and found herself standing by Ben's daughter.

"Naomi." Ben held the teeter-totter level. "This is Daddy's friend, Carlie. Carlie, this is my princess. Naomi."

Naomi hit Carlie with a bold, curious stare. "I'm not a princess, Daddy," she said, eyes on Carlie. "I'm a dragon slayer."

"You know what I think?" Carlie asked Naomi.

"What do you think, Carlie?" She shook her head so hard, wispy curls escaped her braid.

"I think dragon slayers are probably strong enough to slay grubs, too."

Naomi's eyes lit up. She flashed Carlie a grin and looked back at Ben.

"I can slay the grubs, Daddy."

Carlie offered Ben a small grin. "I'd expect nothing less from a warrior's daughter."

"Carlie!" Naomi called. "Get on with me, so Daddy can make us fly."

Ben had made Carlie fly many times since that first kiss. Enthralled by the invitation from Naomi, she climbed on the end of the teeter-totter behind the little girl. She breathed in the scent of baby shampoo and maple syrup and sunshine.

"You have to hold on." Naomi looked at her over her shoulder, her sweet face scrunched in a somber frown.

"I will," Carlie promised her. She reached around Naomi to grab the handle with her and looked at Ben.

"Ready, ladies?" he called.

"Ready!" Carlie and Naomi answered in unison. Naomi burst into giggles. Gaze locked with Ben's, Carlie laughed softly and dropped a kiss on the top of Naomi's head. This was going to be quite a ride.

***THE END***

THANK you so much for reading End in Flames.

IF YOU ENJOYED READING about Carlie and Ben, please consider leaving a review on your favorite book retail site as well as Goodreads or Bookbub.

# RESCUE ME: A HERO ROMANCE COLLECTION

Rescue Me: A Hero Romance Collection

Benefiting Tunnels to Towers a non-profit Foundation that was started to honor the sacrifice of firefighter Stephen Siller, who gave his life saving strangers on September 11, 2001. His organization honors those who have taken an oath to make the supreme sacrifice of life and limb for our country when needed. You can find out more or make a direct donation to Tunnels to Towers by visiting www.t2t.org

Everyone Deserves a *Hero*.

10 Authors have teamed together to bring you these heart-stopping, swoon worthy, hero romance stories

that will leave you breathless. This collection of books are stand-alone stories that will leave you wanting more.

This Hero Romance Collection is dedicated to the extraordinary men and women who put their lives on the line for the ordinary people of this great nation. In recognition of their faithful service, each of the participating authors made a donation to Tunnels to Towers, a non-profit organization, upon joining this Hero Romance Collection.

*This collection includes:*

*Ignition by USA Today Bestselling Authors Lux Miller & LC Taylor* → *https://books2read.com/Ignition*

*Crossing the Line by USA Today Bestselling Author LC Taylor* → *https://books2read.com/CrossingthelineEbook*

*Professional Consult by USA Today Bestselling Author Lark Anderson* → *https://books2read.com/u/m0l92Y*

*Sacrifice by USA Today Bestselling Author Amy Stephens* → *My Book*

*Rescued by Him by USA Today Bestselling Author Ashley Zakrzewski* → *My Book*

*Rocco's Atonement by Award Winning Author E.M. Shue* → *https://books2read.com/RoccosAtonement*

*Sworn to Serve by YD La Mar* → *https://books2read.com/u/4Ap19q*

*End in Flames by Tracy Broemmer* → *https://books2read.com/u/49kX8M*

*Bailed Out by Mary Morano* → *https://books2read.com/Bailedout*

*Burning for Her by Samantha Conley* → *My Book*

***All proceeds from Ignition will be donated to Tunnels to Towers for a minimum of six months. Each author has made a contribution to participate in this multi-author anthology to be donated to the Foundation. It is solely up to them whether or not they donate proceeds from their books.***

# PREVIEW OF BOONE'S GIRL

Chapter 1

Bodhi

Irony at its finest.

Bodhi Reyburn made a left onto Yesterday Avenue and eyeballed the huge, modern building that dominated the newly updated campus. Everything here had either been updated or razed and built new from scratch. Home to stay this time, she pulled into a parking spot in the teacher's lot and sat idle to study the sight.

She didn't hate it. Actually, she liked it. The administration building was front and center, a gorgeous conglomeration of cedar planks and glass. She had been inside the building for her interview, and though she had only gotten a peek at the offices and the computer lab on the first floor, she was excited to get back inside and do some exploring before August nineteenth.

Eyes roaming over the eastern wing of the building that led directly to the just as shiny new middle school building—Bodhi's building—she put the Subaru in park and eased her foot off the brake. As excited as she was about what the new building and technology would offer so many students, she needed a little shot of nostalgia. Seeing the same, old faded brown brick building here on Yesterday Avenue would have been a little slice of comfort for her still partly broken self.

Wasn't just her heart. Ty had broken it, no question, but in the twelve months since her world had come crashing down around her, she'd lost interest in every-thing, including her mental and physical health. In fact, the move home, the new job—all of it—was a last-ditch effort to pull herself out of the depression she hadn't even realized gripped her. If it weren't for her best friend, she might still be wallowing back in that horrid rental that wasn't much more than a glorified closet.

She still missed him.

Maybe she loved him. Maybe some part of Bodhi Reyburn was destined to always love something in Tyson Boone. But she wasn't *in love* with him. Hadn't been for a long time.

In hindsight, she supposed that might have been part of the problem.

Nope. On second thought, no need to see the old LCHS building. Not for comfort. Not for dredging up old memories, good or bad. Bodhi squeezed her hands into fists and rested them on her thighs, swung her gaze back toward the main building and beyond—hello? How many high school campuses had trendy coffee bars?— and sucked in one last deep breath. For courage.

Because she sure as hell needed it.

What had she been thinking when she applied for

this job? Of all the teaching positions available, why had she applied for, interviewed for, and been offered this one? Well, Shay, for one. Her best friend had dragged her out of the rental house daily to either the coffee shop up the street or the wine bar on the corner and searched for jobs with her, as if she was newly sixteen and reluctant to get off her butt and go to work. Naturally, the position at Lake Clair was at the top of the list when they started looking.

*Time to face the music, Bodhi.*

Ignoring the slight tremble in her hands, she climbed out of the car, swung the door closed, and opened the hatchback to grab a milkcrate filled with things for her classroom. She'd tossed her oversized purse in the crate when she left the townhouse, so she closed the hatch and headed up the sidewalk to the administration building. There was nothing of any value in the car—a few sticks of Spearmint gum and an old tube of Chapstick—so she didn't worry about locking up.

"Hey!"

She looked up in time to see a somewhat familiar face headed her way, from the admin building to the lot. Ninety-nine percent sure she'd met the woman when she'd been here to interview, she scoured her brain for a name. And wouldn't you know it? Came up empty. Another side effect of everything with Ty. No focus. No attention to details. Forgetting things.

"Bodhi, right?"

"Yes—"

"Piper," the woman slowed as she neared. "Please.

You're not going to remember half the names here since they combined all the schools into one campus."

True. But if she were being honest, that was one thing that had drawn Bodhi back to Lake Clair. The new campus combined the elementary and middle schools in the eastern wing, while the west wing housed the high school and all the appropriate science, communication, and technology labs, as well as offices for at least four guidance counselors. Bodhi was banking on getting lost in the sea of faces and keeping her nose to the grindstone.

"Piper." She nodded and smiled. No, she didn't want to make friends, but the ghost of the extroverted person she used to be lingered. She had never been rude a day in her life; she wouldn't let her personal issues with Ty change that part of herself.

"Welcome to Lake Clair." Piper lifted her hands as if she was reaching for the milkcrate Bodhi carried. "Need a hand?"

"No, thanks." Bodhi shrugged. "I'm sure you've got plenty to carry in."

Piper stepped away but looked back with a laugh. "Too true. I'm in room six."

Okay, so the bubbly redhead made Bodhi think of Shay. Her best friend was sweet and compassionate and would totally offer to help rearrange and decorate someone else's classroom before finishing her own. They looked a bit alike, too. Same slim, petite build, though Shay was a brown-eyed blonde.

"Four," Bodhi told the woman.

"Great. I'll check on you in a bit."

Bodhi made her way through the admin building, took the hall on the right that led to the covered outdoor walkway to the middle school building and eventually, the elementary classrooms. Luckily, she made it to her classroom without running into anyone else. At the door, she put the crate down and tugged her keys from the pocket of her jeans. Piper was nice, but Bodhi couldn't afford niceness right now. She needed all of her energy, her focus, for recovering herself.

Open door resting against her shoulder, she reached to the left and flipped the light switch. She stood just for a moment, taking it in. Under the bright lights, every flat surface in the room sparkled. No one, save for the construction workers and yeah, probably the administration, had been inside this room. No teachers had stood at the podium in the front, no students had written on these desks, no dry erase markers had touched the whiteboards.

Brand-spanking new.

For a moment, she was a hundred and fifty miles away, standing on the threshold of a very different space, very different life. Not new. They couldn't afford new things, but the house was cute, very clean. In fact, for just a second, Bodhi swore she could smell the stringent cleaning agent she had smelled then in the tiny little kitchen.

*Yeah, well, get out the mind bleach, Bodhi.*

Leaning back into the hallway, she picked the crate up and carried it into her room. When the pneumatic door closed slowly behind her, she glanced back, wondering if she should prop it open. She didn't want to appear standoffish to her new colleagues. Even if she totally *wanted to be* one hundred percent standoffish.

With a shrug, she let it go for now and toted the crate to the gray metal desk at the front of the room. Her desk. *Ms. Reyburn.* Once upon a time, she had loved being a teacher. Moving back home, taking this job at Lake Clair, would hopefully bring back the joy she found in the classroom.

She curled her fingers around her purse and pulled it out of the crate. Dropping it to the desk, she dug into the crate of books. So much she had to do to get ready for the school year, but of course, she brought the books in first. They'd always been important to her, never more so than when things went so far south with Ty.

*The Hunger Games. Peter and the Star Catchers. Bud, Not Buddy. The Boy in the Striped Pajamas. Esperanza Rising.*

Bodhi had read them all and hundreds more at least twice, if not more. She'd read Maggie Stiefvater's Raven Cycle books again just this year. Nothing like burying your head—heart—in a beloved book to get through the hard times.

*Hard times.*

Bodhi yanked the chair out from under her desk and dropped into it. The books piled in front of her, she turned her head to look out the wall of windows to her right. The L shaped building that was home to the classrooms framed a beautiful quad where students and teachers alike would be encouraged to soak up the sun and fresh air in between classes and over lunch periods.

Right now, she was too exhausted, too numb, too

everything and nothing all at once, to notice the flower beds and the park benches placed throughout the quad. Maybe eventually, she would find herself, her strength, and then the beauty out there. For now, she simply focused on breathing.

Because even that much hurt.

***

If you'd like to continue reading about Bodhi and Will, click here:

books2read.com/boonesgirl

# About the Author

Tracy is the author of the contemporary romance series the H Books—Gettin' Hitched, Hookin' Up, and Holdin' On and the Mississippi Queen Trilogy. Tracy also writes women's fiction and is the author of the Williams Legacy series as well as several stand-alone titles.

Tracy's books have been called gripping, emotional, and timely, and readers describe her characters as real and relatable.

Tracy lives in Midwestern Illinois with her husband of 29 years.

Learn more about Tracy and her books:

www.broemmerbooks.com

# ALSO BY TRACY BROEMMER

Women's Fiction Novels:

Luther's Cross 10th Anniversary Edition

Fairytale (Writing as Therese Kinkaide)

Just Like Them

Small Hours

Picket Fences

Two Story Home

Green-Eyed Girl

Say Everything

Come Home For Christmas

Sketching Litchfield Lake

Ever, Again

Safe as Houses

Damsel

The Valentine Suite

Every Little Thing, Lorelei Bluffs, Book 1

Two A.M., Lorelei Bluffs, Book 2

Blind, Lorelei Bluffs, Book 3

Leaving July, Lorelei Bluffs, Book 4

Hesitation Marks, Lorelei Bluffs, Book 5

Gettin' Hitched, The H Books, Book 1

Hookin' Up, The H Books, Book 2

Holdin' On, The H Books, Book 2.5


Contemporary Romance Novellas:

Indian Summer, A Novella

Dear Jaclyn Perris, A Novella

French Stuff, A Novella, Originally included in newsletter builder anthology, Just Coffee

Holdin' On, A Novella, Originally published in the anthology, Snowed Inn


Other Novellas:

The Devy Man, A Horror Novella


Women's Fiction Short Stories:

India Falls

Luther's Cross: 87,600

The Candy Cane Tree of Willow Lane

Delays, Originally published in the anthology, Snowed Inn, Vol.2

Same Time Next Year, Published in the anthology, Sweet Sprinkles

Contemporary Romance Short Stories:

Perfect Pictures, The Wine Tasting Series, Traminette

Coming Home, The Wine Tasting Series, Edelweiss

Save Me Every Dance, The Wine Tasting Series, Rosé

Marry Me, The Wine Tasting Series, Shiraz

Birthday Wishes, The Wine Tasting Series, Muscat

Dad Jeans, The Wine Tasting Series, Vignoles

Peppermint Lane, Originally published in the anthology, Sweet Treats